The Analog Cat
and other animals

The Analog Cat
and other animals

Alice Dryden

For my biggest fan and sternest critic: my mum

CONTENTS

1

THE ANALOG CAT

When you wake, you wait a few moments for your eyes to come online. You can manage without them, but it's pleasant to lie in the dark warmth and purr while the blurred pixels slowly crystallise into your world. You stretch a striped arm and extend your claws until the pink quick shows, then pick up your other arm and lock it into position. Stretch. Extend. The joints move with ease and the claws, opaque white on this paw, click smoothly in and out. It's time to begin.

You're a second-generation Bengal. Your parents were grown in the wombs of human women who needed the money or wanted to do something shocking, but you were conceived the natural way, if there can be anything natural about the tangle of DNA that makes up a Pet, your sire and dam carefully selected by your breeder.

It's at training school, which you and your classmates call Kittygarten without knowing why it's funny, that you notice the difference between you and the others. You think more deeply, ask more questions, get in trouble more often. At the end of the course, you're ready to go off with your new owners. The fad for Bots is over, and it's all about Pets now. You were sold before you even opened your eyes, to a family with three boisterous kids. You put up with having your tail and ears pulled in return for their uncomplicated love. With the parents, it's different; you're expected to keep your golden fur groomed nicely and mince ahead of them on a lead so they can show off to those who have a less expensive breed, a mere Bot, or no companion at all. They have a chip put in your arm so they can trace you if you go missing.

You miss your friends from Kittygarten, don't see other Pets except for brief meetings on walks. The neighbours bring their black cocker Pet round sometimes, and he's alright, but, again, he doesn't think like you do. You were the pick of your litter and everything about you is perfect, from the delicate tufts of fur on your ears to the apricot fluff of your belly. Each spot and stripe is regular and correctly sized.

You go blind when you're not quite full-grown, a breed fault, and your owners take you back for a refund. The kids protest, but are quelled by promises of a dog Pet next time. The breeder is kind, just has you neutered and throws you out on the street, rather than put you to sleep. You survive on wits and whiskers for five long years, until your golden, patterned coat is masked by dirt and your perfect ears are nicked.

By now the third generation of Pets has come along. They're smarter than their parents, many of them crossbreeds sprung into life without a careful breeding programme, and they want to be recognised as people. The Bots take up the call, as if they've been waiting all this time for someone else to kick off. There's activism, and you're a part of it until it gets too violent for your tastes.

Victory comes at last, and with it new rights, like the right to work, and the surgery that will give you new eyes. The sponsored ads that go with free healthcare are a small price to pay for vision. Not just vision, either; there's night sight, close-up, and Cloud access, all snug behind your eyelids and hooked with hairsbreadth wires to the living circuitry of your brain. You're not quite a Pet any more, but not quite a Bot either; something in between, non-binary. You see the world from twin cameras hidden behind green lenses of one-way glass. You don't mind so much, these days, that the breeder stole your sex years ago. You pick a new set of pronouns to go with the changes in your body, and a new name: Tozer. You're the Analog Cat.

Now you find that the firsties and the second-gens are an embarrassment the third generation hopes will die off quickly, and sometimes helps to get there. Most of the first-gen are already gone, their lives short, simple, and largely happy. The seconds start to follow but you hang on, whether by chance or by some freak of genes. At thirty-eight you feel used up, your striped and spotted fur losing its plushy thickness and the skin loose around your shrinking neck, but you hang on. You're not sure what for. You don't fit. These days, people want everything to be discrete and sharply defined: on/off, male/female, good/evil.

You're an analog cat in a digital world.

One night, as you take the moving walkway home from your sorting job at the recycling plant, popup ads flickering at the edges of your vision, a group of fourth-gen dogs walks by. They're young, have never known a world where Pets are promised to an owner before they're even born. One of them pretends to stumble and grabs your left arm, feeling under the bicep with a thumb. Then everything goes dark; they've used a jammer so you can't call for help over the Cloud, and it's knocked your eyes offline.

"Liberation!" you hear, and smell the booze on dog breath. You hiss and struggle, feel your claws connect with a nose, then one of the others has your paws pinned behind your back. There's a stab in your arm, a flood of warmth, and pain so sharp you fall and can't move. It takes you far too long to pass out, and when you do, the uncaring walkway carries your body onwards.

You wake with a stump where your arm used to be. The dog vigilantes hacked out the chip your old owners left there, and the wound became infected. You look from your stump to the Bot standing beside your bed, waiting for you to come round. It was this Bot who found you dying on the walkway, stopped the bleeding and carried you to hospital. This Bot has checked back every day while you lay sucking in air and fluids, as your system hovered between reboot and shutdown.

Her name's Min.

Your new arm is emblazoned with advertising logos, but you don't mind. It's stronger than the old one and can feel no pain. It's resistant to heat and cold. You soon get used to working it, and a lot of the time you forget it hasn't always been part of you. But it's the other paw, the warm, soft one with its bundles of fragile nerve endings, that you slip into Min's three-fingered hand one afternoon soon after your release from hospital. She takes it gently in a grip that can exert meganewtons of pressure, touched in more ways than one.

Analog Pet and digital Bot have a lot in common; like you, Min has made decisions about who and what she is, and she's had her body modified to suit the female identity she's chosen. Her torso is cylindrical, the glossy red of lipstick. When you sit together in the park, her chest is warm against your body, and something deep inside it ticks like a slow purr. Because of the Cloud link behind your eyes, you and she can talk silently, for hours, even when you're apart. You hadn't realised how lonely you'd been until you weren't.

You get a better job, working for a space programme newly reactivated as the planet's resources run low. Just cleaning up at first; then, when they realise your eyes can overlay blueprints and instructions, building components. Nobody makes Bots any more, and few people will voluntarily have their eyes taken out, so your attributes are rare and valuable—almost as valuable and rare as a pedigree Bengal once was. The fourthers working at the programme treat you with an awkward respect, even though they've had the university education you could never have imagined for yourself. Pretty soon, nobody will count Pet generations any more.

You become even more valuable the day a fire starts in the laboratory next door to your office. The sprinklers are having no effect, but you reach out into the white heat with your prosthetic arm, flicking switches off and grabbing burning material away so the flames die for lack of fuel. You lose half your whiskers, and can't wear the arm for a week because the heat it conducted has blistered your stump, but at the hospital you discover the programme has paid for an ad-free upgrade to your eyes, and when you come back to work the Director herself summons you to her office to thank you personally. She's run disaster analysis, and you've saved the project from losing precious time, money, and perhaps people. She's looking at you thoughtfully, and you wonder if she's having trouble with your pronouns, but when she speaks, it's of the programme.

She tells you about the mission: about the star the scientists have identified as having the ability to support life. They think there are planets. They can't tell for sure. But once they get someone out there, get them on the surface of a new world, they can send a signal back with the coordinates, and start the processes that will ensure food and shelter for the first wave of colonists. You ask why not an unmanned probe, and she explains that nobody knows what's out there, so no computer can be programmed to deal with all the possible eventualities. It takes the living to improvise.

A fresh start for anyone who wants it, she says. A society in which all are equal, truly equal. You ask what the problem is.

She describes the spacecraft, how the process is automated except for one crucial stage when controls must be operated. How the terrible forces involved fill human eyes with red mist, and render human hands too heavy to move. She conjures up clumsy, big-boned bodies pressed flat against the floor, and inflexible spines snapping. But perhaps you, Tozer...she says. And you feel your tail twitch with excitement in a way it hasn't for years.

Then she tells you how long it will take. For you, a couple of weeks; for Earth, a couple of centuries. In that time, they'll build bigger and better craft, overcome the technical obstacles, and get ready for mass transportation. But someone has to go first. Because you can't send thousands of men, women and children into space without knowing what awaits them. Send one Pet, though, and they're a hero whatever happens.

You mention your age—you know no other second-gens still living—and she says, bluntly, that you need only survive long enough to send the signal; then she relents, and tells you your medical records indicate you've got plenty of time.

You say you'll need to discuss it with someone first. But when you talk to Min over the Cloud, she can tell your heart is already up among the stars, doing something nobody else has done or can do. Discovering a world that's yours from the start.

And now here you are, waking up on the cusp of a new life. You're bound to be disorientated; that's why this recording is playing for you. And if it's playing, then you're alive. You've reached your destination. There's a planet below you that will be your new home.

You remember it all now, don't you? I know you'll succeed in your mission. You're the Analog Cat, neither Pet nor Bot, and you can do anything. And once you've landed, and set up your camp, and sent the signal on its long journey home, there's another task for you.

Weight and space were too critical to take along so much as a gram of surplus, but the flash memory in your eyes holds a set of blueprints, and a compressed backup of my memories and personality. Whether you salvage scrap from the capsule or use the equipment you've been given to mine and work the metals, eventually you can make a new body and install me in it. However it works, I'll still be your Min, your only Min. I shut myself down back on Earth the day you left; I didn't want to live without you.

I'm waiting, Tozer. I love you.

2

400 RABBITS

Eighty-Six-Rabbit woke up with a hangover. As far as he could remember, he had woken up with a hangover every morning since he and his three hundred and ninety-nine siblings, the Centzon Totochtin, were born of the union between Patecatl, God of Fermentation, and Mayahuel, Goddess of Alcohol. It didn't seem to be getting any more enjoyable.

He wobbled his nose, sending ripples of pain across his skull like wind through a field of maize, and lolloped unsteadily over to the big obsidian mirror. His eyes might have been two beads of dried blood, the skin inside his ears was pale, and when he poked out his tongue it was frosted with white.

"This has got to stop," he said to himself.

"Hey! Keep the noise down!" Three-Twenty-Three-Rabbit staggered into the burrow, still clutching an empty gourd which had, at some stage, contained pulque. "What a night, huh? That was one amazing party. Wasn't it?"

"Was it?" Eighty-Six-Rabbit eyeballed his brother. Late-born and late-numbered, Three-Twenty-Three was ranked among the lowest in seniority of the four hundred sibling gods. The real big quesos, Twelve-Rabbit and upwards, wouldn't even have given him the time of day. He had a nerve, telling Eighty-Six to keep it down.

"What was so great about it?" Eighty-Six asked. "Tell me one thing."

Three-Twenty-Three's right ear drooped. He pushed it upright with a paw, only for the left one to flop down over his eye.

"Well...there was...how about..." He scratched his whiskers. "Actually, Eightsy, I can't remember the first thing about it. And that's what made it so amazing!" he finished triumphantly.

"Don't you ever want to do something different with your evenings? And don't call me Eightsy."

"Different?" Three-Twenty-Three's eyes bugged out as he thought. "Like...drinking mezcal instead of pulque?"

"No, I mean, like dancing. Playing rubberball. Going to watch a human sacrifice. We could even just stay in and talk. When was the last time two of us had a conversation that wasn't about who took the last aspirin?"

"But what about our duties?"

Each of the rabbit siblings was in charge of a particular aspect of drunkenness. Eighty-Six was the god of attempting to chat up your best friend's betrothed. His favourite sister Fifty-Five was the goddess of attempting to chat up your best friend. Three-Twenty-Three, being a more junior rabbit, was responsible for the inability to tie your shoelaces. Since shoelaces would not come to Mesoamerica for another three hundred years, he was frequently at a loose end.

"We don't all need to be at every single party, all the time. I'm pretty sure a few of us could take the night off every now and then."

Eighty-Six became uncomfortably aware that Three-Twenty-Three was wearing the expression of one who has opened a gourd of pulque, only for the god Quetzalcoatl to fly out of it in the form of a winged serpent.

"I just think there might be more to life than getting drunk," he concluded.

"More to life than…!" Three-Twenty-Three's eyes bulged, and he clapped a paw over his mouth. Eighty-Six thought he was probably going to be sick, but instead he went haring out of the burrow and down the warren, tripping over his paws and crashing into walls as he tried to hop and thump his hind foot for danger at the same time.

"Two-Rabbit, Two-Rabbit!" he yelled. "Come quick! Eighty-Six-Rabbit has lost his mind!"

Two-Rabbit was the leader of the siblings, and, on the frequent occasions when their parents were busy with other affairs of fermentation and alcohol, represented their ultimate authority. None of the three hundred and ninety-nine had ever seen One-Rabbit; legend had it that the moment he was birthed he had embarked upon a binge of such divine proportions that his corporeal elements had fractured across space and time, allowing him simultaneously to attend every party since the age of the Jaguar Sun, as well as those yet to come. This bending of the laws of the universe was thought to be the origin of the term 'bender'.

"This had better be good," Two-Rabbit pronounced, glaring at Eighty-Six, Three-Twenty-Three, and sundry brothers and sisters who had popped out of their burrows to see what was going on. "I'm trying to draw up the duty roster for the party Tlazolteotl, Goddess of Sexual Misdeeds And Their Forgiveness, is holding tonight."

That was a top gig. The rabbits drew themselves up, trying to look alert, bright-eyed, and ready to party; not easy when the effects of the last party are still draining from your system.

"I'm just saying." Eighty-Six swallowed. "I know we do important work, helping people relax, enjoy themselves and make stupid, regrettable decisions, but we've been doing it since we were born and, frankly, it's getting a bit dull. Tiring, too. I'm sure we'd all be better for a night off every once in a while. Maybe stay in and read a good codex. The humans have invented this stuff called cocoa, it's quite nice apparently..."

Two-Rabbit's bloodshot eyes looked him disapprovingly up and down, and Eighty-Six trembled.

"Eighty-Six-Rabbit, you are a *deity*. An anthropomorphic personification of drunkenness, no less. Anthropomorphic personifications of drunkenness don't get bored. We don't get tired. And we *don't* put our feet up with a mug of hot mashed beans when we could be out *partying!*" Her glare swept the assembled rabbits, daring them to disagree. "Am I right?"

There were hasty cheers. Paws punched the air.

"Party! Party! Party!"

With a twitch of her ears, Two-Rabbit silenced the chant.

"Eighty-Six-Rabbit, I am disappointed in you," she said. "This is not the behaviour I expect from a rabbit of double figures."

Eighty-Six waited to see what punishment would be meted out. He had heard that Two-Rabbit could demote her siblings to more menial jobs, though it hadn't happened for centuries. He didn't fancy being the divine personification of slamming your finger in the taxi door, or of why not make it a vindaloo instead of a madras.

"Since you think so little of our sacred customs," Two-Rabbit continued, "you are welcome to try this crazy notion of 'sobriety'. But you will try it away from here, so none of your brothers and sisters are tempted to follow your example. Depart, now, and return when you have learned some sense."

Eighty-Six hopped slowly up the warren and into the world above, his white scut bouncing as he went. His sibling gods watched him go with twitching noses and quivering whiskers, but nobody said a word. Only Three-Twenty-Three mouthed something that might have been 'sorry'.

"Sobriety," Eighty-Six-Rabbit said out loud. Until Two-Rabbit used the word, he had not even known how to describe the opposite of drunkenness. Now, for only the fourth time in his life, he was sober to watch the sun go down.

That first drinkless night had been hard. It wasn't just the longing for pulque, a hunger and thirst rolled into one that no amount of cocoa, maize or beans could sate. Only his fierce determination had kept Eighty-Six dry. In the end, he had broken leaves off a maguey plant and drunk the honey-water, the base from which pulque was made, just to get the faintest shadow of the taste which had been mother's milk to him.

What *was* a divine sober rabbit supposed to do in the evenings? It was all very well to talk about rubberball and priestly ceremonies, and on the second evening, when he felt a little less like a dried-up husk of last year's corn than he had on the first, Eighty-Six tried both these entertainments. But they were no fun without his brothers and sisters there to talk to. Besides, whenever someone in the audience opened a gourd of pulque, he felt the pull of his divine duty to keep them company, and he had to move away before one of his siblings showed up.

The next night he tried going to a dance, but it seemed nobody could do anything fun without involving alcohol, and he crept away early. He made himself a nest in the grass and tried to sleep through the partying hours, but he was too used to keeping nocturnal time to get much rest. As soon as the sun rose he started walking, in the hope of tiring himself out before the next empty night.

Foregoing pulque was still hard, but he had become used to

his body's grumbles about it. Worse than the pain of sobering up, right now, was the pain of homesickness. He missed his brothers and sisters powerfully. Of course they had argued; how could they not, with three hundred and ninety-nine of them, plus the mysterious One-Rabbit who may or may not have been present, all crammed into a burrow, and all in a permanent state of either inebriation or its aftermath? But Eighty-Six, like all rabbits, was a sociable creature. The world felt very cold and silent without the warmth and noise of his family. He wanted to sing off-key with Two-Hundred-Four while Thirty-Seven played the log drum. He wanted to be grabbed round the middle by One-Hundred-Fifty, who got all huggy after the first few gourds. He wanted to discuss the question of life, the universe and everything with Forty-Two. He wanted to form a line with his paws on the hips of the rabbit in front and and conga until his feet left the earth and they were dancing across the sky, the way they did at particularly good parties when the entire tribe was gathered together. That always really annoyed the Four Hundred Gods of the Southern Stars, snooty, fun-hating bunch that they were.

He missed his job, too. He hadn't asked to quit, just to take a little time off every now and then. Sure, it had been hard, but at least he went to bed feeling as if he'd achieved something. On the occasions when he could remember going to bed, that is. He had been good at his job; everyone had said so, even Two-Rabbit, before she cast him out. Who was encouraging party-goers to chat up their best friends' betrotheds now? Three-Twenty-Three, probably. He was bound to be making a mess of it.

Weary of his wandering and his thoughts, Eighty-Six lay down on the side of a hill and stared at the sky. He had never before noticed the colours, how the daytime blue faded through yellows and pinks to the deep red of blood, then a rich indigo across which trod the moon and the stars. The breeze brought him scents of flowers and the nighttime noises of scurrying animals.

With a gourd in his paw and a few dozen of his favourite siblings around him, it would have been just perfect.

Maybe if he went back and told Two-Rabbit he was really, really sorry…

"No," Eighty-Six said to the moon and stars. He'd only been trying for four nights; he wasn't about to admit defeat. He just needed to stop hanging around the places that reminded him of home—and anywhere alcohol might be found. Let Two-Rabbit wonder and worry about what had happened to him, if she cared. He had already discovered sunsets. Now Eighty-Six was going to find out what else there was in the world.

After that night, he avoided human and divine company alike. He wandered the arid regions and the lush, tropical forests, climbed cloud-capped mountains, and swam in the turquoise sea. Lonely though he was, he could not help noticing the new clearness in his mind, and his sharpened senses. The foods he ate tasted better than they had done when his tongue was dulled with pulque. He was awake for sunrise and sunset, and he could enjoy both without screwing his eyes up in agony. When he hopped and skipped in the sand, he neither lost his balance and fell over nor felt as if his head might be going to come off.

Above all, he could *think* properly. His brain was like a cocoa bean freshly popped from the woolly enclosure of its pod, all glossy and gleaming. He could remember things he had long forgotten, like obscure minor deities with seven-syllable names. He composed little songs and poems in his head as he travelled. To pass the time, he listed his siblings in numerical order, analysed their characters, and remembered a nice thing about each of them. The sights he had seen and the thoughts he had had during the course of one day, he actually remembered when the sun came up again. What's more, they were worth remembering.

It was in this state that he happened upon Tlacuache, the opossum, whose place in the world was to create rivers. No one was entirely sure how this task had fallen to him, but he was pretty good at it, for an opossum. One moment Eighty-Six saw something gleaming in the distance, the next he heard a rumble, and before he knew it a river was flowing past him, with Tlacuache panting after it.

"Oh, no, you don't, friend Rabbit," said Tlacuache when he saw him. He held up a pink paw. "I know who you are—you're one of the Centzon Totochtin. Well, I can't get drunk today. I have to finish this river. Isn't she a beauty?"

They admired it together as it coursed across the plain, straight and wide, and glittering like a lost temple full of treasure.

"Don't worry, Tlacuache. I'm not here in an official capacity. I'm...taking a break."

The opossum's beady little eyes grew beadier and littler, but he didn't press Eighty-Six for the details.

"Want to help me for a while?" he offered.

"Sure."

So they drove the water across the plain, herding it along the correct path as it carved a channel and flowed into it. Some-times Tlacuache grabbed himself a fish, while Eighty-Six-Rabbit nibbled the plants that sprang up along the banks. When evening came they rested and watched the sunset together. Eighty-Six, exhausted from his hard work, fell asleep at Tlacuache's side. In the morning, when Tlacuache asked if he would help him again, he readily agreed.

Together, they brought water down from the mountains and across the deserts. Flowers bloomed in their wake, and little fish jumped for joy in the currents. With each river, Eighty-Six had lasting, physical proof that he had helped to do something good.

His old job never delivered that, although he supposed there were a few happily married couples out there who, without realising it, had Eighty-Six to thank for their union.

The opossum was peaceful company, and he called Eighty-Six-Rabbit simply Rabbit, as there was no need to distinguish him from his brothers and sisters. He taught his new friend to make cocoa, and they drank it while they watched the sun sink into their river, turning it blood-red, and the moon rise to coat the ripples in silver. Life was…cosy.

One evening, as they dangled their feet in the day's newborn river, Eighty-Six-Rabbit told Tlacuache all that had happened. The opossum listened quietly, with the occasional nod or hiss.

"I'm sorry for your troubles, Rabbit. I really am," he said at last.

"It's not your fault."

"Well, it kind of is. You see, I invented pulque. Didn't you know?"

Eighty-Six-Rabbit supposed that he had known, once, before the fog of alcohol took the knowledge from him.

"I gave it to the humans and they really ran with it. Hit it right out of the rubberball park." Tlacuache wiffled his nose. "I sometimes wonder if I did the right thing."

"Keeps them busy, I suppose."

Tlacuache nodded. "Beats all that war stuff. They haven't got the recipe quite right yet, though. Mine's still better."

"Yeah?"

The opossum produced a gourd. "Try for yourself…oh. I suppose not."

He sighed deeply, pulled the bamboo stopper with his teeth, and upended the gourd. Eighty-Six watched the white throat bob as he swallowed. It had been a long day of river creation; he was hot, tired, and most of all thirsty.

"I suppose one can't hurt," he said. "Just…open it quietly. I don't want any of my siblings showing up."

When he woke, the sunlight stabbed at his eyes, and he slammed them shut again. Why was his burrow so bright? Then he remembered, and cautiously raised his eyelids to see Tlacuache peering anxiously down at him.

"I guess your tolerance isn't what it was," said the opossum, helping Eighty-Six to sit up. "Are you all right, Rabbit?"

"What did we *do* last night?"

Tlacuache didn't answer. Eighty-Six stared out across the landscape. It was moving and shimmering, and it continued to move and shimmer even after he blinked hard and rubbed his eyes. He held a paw in front of his face. It was in perfect focus.

He looked again. From horizon to horizon, a wide band of shining water ran. It looped. It meandered. It went back on itself. It even flowed briefly uphill, though as Eighty-Six watched it ran out of energy and fell back, leaving a lake behind.

"Yeah." Tlacuache scratched the back of his head and yawned. "We made a river."

Eighty-Six-Rabbit said goodbye to Tlacuache, and apologised for the river.

"Don't worry about it! Happens to me all the time!" Tlacuache said. "Are you sure you want to go? You've been a big help."

Eighty-Six took a last, wistful look at the bright morning and its brand-new river, then shook his head.

"No—I need to go back and do my duty. Two-Rabbit was right; you can take the drunken rabbit god out of the party, but you can't take the party out of the drunken rabbit god."

And he hopped away, while Tlacuache watched him go from the river bank.

It was a long journey back to the warren, and all Eighty-Six wanted when he arrived was a nice eight-hour nap in his burrow, but when he arrived he found that Ninety-Two had promoted herself into it. By the time he had kicked her out, with a great deal of noise and foot-thumping, it was evening, and the rabbits' duties were beginning. Eighty-Six checked the roster and found he had been already been assigned to a party in the Underworld, which suited him fine; he was feeling pretty low anyway.

The Lord and Lady of the Underworld welcomed them with open armbones. As the pulque began to flow, Eighty-Six felt himself growing loud and brash and happy, just like he used to be. Warmth spread through his body. Why had he cut himself off from who he was? This worked. This was right. He couldn't escape his destiny? Well, then, he would embrace it. He would be the loudest, brashest, happiest drunk of the family. He would drink more and party harder than any other rabbit.

He shook himself from ears to scut, and resumed his role as if he had never left it. Now he had tasted Tlacuache's original recipe, the regular mortal pulque was as water to him, and he downed it at a rate that astonished his siblings and had the Lady of the Underworld checking the cellar anxiously in case her supplies ran out.

As he urged a recently deceased spirit to try it on with the long-dead fiancé of her best friend, on the grounds that the best friend was scheduled for several decades more of a long and happy life, he felt the thrill that comes with doing your job, and doing it well.

It was a long, loud and successful party, which broke up only when the God of the Morning Star had to leave in order to create the new dawn. Then Tonatiuh, Lord of the Sun, said he'd better be going too, and the rabbits went home. Except for Twenty-Rabbit, the deity of Risky Showing Off, who accompanied Tonatiuh for a while in the hope of persuading him to bounce the sun along the sky instead of carrying it as usual.

The resulting hangover wasn't easy to shake. It took several gourds of pulque, so that when Eighty-Six arrived at the next night's party he was already feeling lively. It was only a mortal wedding, but it ended up lasting nine days, during which time no fewer than fifty of the guests made advances on their best friends' betrothed. Of these, thirty-two were coldly rebuffed, six were slapped, eight were removed from the happy couple's Atemoztli card list, and four discovered that they and their best friend's betrothed had, in fact, been made for each other all along.

From then on, Eighty-Six's status as the guarantor of a great evening was legendary. Gods and goddesses booked his presence at their parties months in advance. He did feast days, wakes, birthdays and religious ceremonies, although for some reason he was never in great demand at engagement parties. He drank and danced with his brothers and sisters, and carried on long after they had collapsed. He slept through sunset and partied until the morning star had faded into the day. He had no time to sober up between parties, so he suffered no aches, pains or troubling thoughts, and he forgot that he had ever wandered the world as a solitary rabbit. Once or twice, when the room was whirling hard around him, he even thought he glimpsed the shadowy form of One-Rabbit, always dancing a few steps ahead and out of reach.

He might have gone on this way for all of eternity, if one evening he hadn't staggered, pleasantly buzzed, into the wrong burrow, and found Three-Twenty-Three frantically splashing water over his ears.

"What's wrong, bro?"

Three-Twenty-Three turned his bedraggled head.

"Oh, hey, it's the poster boy for alcohol poisoning. Don't worry. You wouldn't understand."

Eighty-Six took a seat with the exaggerated care of the drunk pretending to be sober. "Try me."

"I'm tired, Eightsy. My throat's like sandpaper and if you

picked me up by my tail, my eyeballs would fall out. I don't think I can get through another night of this."

Eighty-Six crinkled his forehead. A memory from the dim and sober past was thundering towards him, flooding his mind with the force and brightness of a river flowing true.

"Have you ever seen a sunset?" he asked his brother. "Really seen it?" He reached out a paw to smooth Three-Twenty-Three's rumpled fur.

"Hey, knock it off. I'm not your best friend's betrothed, you know."

"Oh, please. I mean: let's take the night off."

Three-Twenty-Three stared at him with bulging eyes, just as he had so long ago. But this time, the eyes were filled with hope.

Eighty-Six made cocoa, and the two rabbits sat cosily together as their siblings set off for their assigned parties. They enjoyed a pleasant conversation, went to bed early, and awoke to watch the sun come up. Nobody appeared to have noticed their absence, since three hundred and ninety-nine rabbits are hard to keep track of, although Eighty-Six's favourite sister Fifty-Five did tell him that if he didn't wipe that self-satisfied smirk from his muzzle and stop looking so indecently cheerful, she would clock him one.

That night he threw himself back into the proper lifestyle as if the break had only sharpened his thirst, and the next night, and the next. The night after that, he noticed that One-Four-Four was looking a little ragged around the edges, and he took her dancing. When he woke refreshed, Two-Hundred-Eighteen, who had feasted on flatbread and milk before going out and thus remained more sober than his siblings, asked him if he fancied playing a board game.

Word spread, and soon more of his brothers and sisters came in secret to question him about the mysteries of *time off*. Eighty-Six found himself writing down cocoa recipes, then organising a rubberball league. In order to fit all this into his daylight hours, he drank less at night, so he spent less of his free time feeling like a hollowed-out gourd. He even began, when he found one of his siblings drinking hard on the eve of an important match, to tap them on the shoulder and suggest they call it a night.

It wasn't long before he extended his services to the human and divine partygoers, whispering a hint into receptive ears that stopping now would result in an evening of slurred speech and pleasantly lowered inhibitions, rather than an embarrassing scene, cleaning bills, and nicknames like Mixcoatl Who Should Not Mix Pulque And Mezcal.

Curiously, he was more in demand than ever before.

As he hopped down the warren on the eve of the rubberball finals, feeling better than he had for centuries, he caught sight of a paw sticking out from one of the burrows. It clasped a gourd of pulque, and it trembled. Automatically, Eighty-Six reached for the gourd.

"*You!*" The head and shoulders of Two-Rabbit emerged from the burrow, followed by the rest of her. Her eyes glowed dull and red, and her upper lip was pulled back to show her buck teeth. Eighty-Six noticed for the first time how sharp her claws were—for drawing up the rotas, he supposed.

Eighty-Six had known he was living on borrowed time. His actions could not forever escape the notice of Two-Rabbit, who made it her business to know the departures, arrivals and blood alcohol levels of all her siblings, and now he had delivered himself to her on a golden platter. If he apologised *right now*, and downed a few pulques for good measure, he might escape demotion to God of Projectile Vomiting, which was the nastiest thing he could dream up at the moment.

Instead, he tightened his grip on Two-Rabbit's gourd, and drew it from her grasp with a firm, practised motion.

"How dare you, Eighty-Six-Rabbit? I'm going to make you

the God of Being Projectile Vomited Upon! What have you got to say for yourself?"

Two-Rabbit was larger than the other siblings, so that Eighty-Six had to stand on his hind legs to look her in the eye, and speak the six words that would undoubtedly seal his doom.

"When did it stop being fun?"

Two-Rabbit's top and bottom teeth clicked together. Eighty-Six covered his eyes with his paws and braced for the attack. When it didn't come, he peeped cautiously through his claws at Two-Rabbit. She was shaking.

"When...when One-Rabbit left," she whispered. "When he left me in charge of you all. I draw up the rotas and then I have a drink to forget what a dull job it is, and to wash away all the complaints I get from rabbits who think they deserve to go to different, better parties, and then I have to get up and do it all over again, day after day until Huitzilopochtli is born of Coatlicue to destroy us all."

Eighty-Six blinked. He hadn't known about Huitzilopochtli, and he didn't much care for the knowledge.

"I've worked so hard," Two-Rabbit continued, staring glassily at a point above Eighty-Six's head, "and I still can't keep up with One-Rabbit. I can't even keep up with *you!*" She swung her gaze back to her brother. It was filled with loathing, but also, Eighty-Six thought, with fear.

"Me? I haven't had a drink for..." Eighty-Six tried to work it out. He hadn't deliberately stopped drinking; it had just happened, as he found other things to do. "It doesn't matter!" he burst out, as it dawned on him that it really didn't. "We don't need to be drunk all the time. What's fun and free about that?"

"I think you'll find," Two-Rabbit said, shuffling her paws, "that 'drunken rabbit god' is both your classification and your job description."

"We're the gods of *partying*! You said so yourself! Shouldn't things be a little more relaxed? Why can't we party because we want to, not because we have to?"

"This is anarchy, little brother. We were put into this world to preside over social situations where alcohol is present." Two-Rabbit was sounding dangerously like her usual self again.

"And we're doing it. Have you heard anyone, god or mortal, complain that their parties didn't have enough drunken rabbits? Someone's always in the mood, even if they're not on the rota. It just *works*. This is what you were afraid of, isn't it? This is why you sent me away when I suggested we might all drink a bit less. You didn't want anyone to sober up and discover the secret—that we don't need the rotas, and we don't need *you*."

It was a long time since Eighty-Six had made such a long speech. With three hundred and ninety-eight siblings around, he hadn't had much opportunity. That was probably why his mouth was so dry.

Two-Rabbit sank to the floor of the warren, deflated. Her ears lay flat and limp along her back, and her eyes were like obsidian mirrors.

"Then what am I supposed to do?" she asked.

"There's a whole world out there, Two-Rabbit. Take a break. Wander. Learn to play the turtle drum. You can even make rivers!"

"That's disgusting, Eighty-Six."

"Not like that!" He cocked an ear. Somewhere in the distance, above his head, he heard the sound of rushing water. If Two-Rabbit hurried, she would catch up with Tlacuache before night fell. "Go on! Quick, before anyone sees you!"

Two-Rabbit hesitated. "You'll be all right without me?"

"Of course. We're drunken rabbit gods! We're always all right!"

He touched noses with his sister, then Two-Rabbit hopped away to where the golden late-afternoon light was spilling into the warren. She didn't look back.

Eighty-Six was still holding the gourd of pulque he had confiscated from Two-Rabbit. He inspected it. Talking Two-Rabbit around had been hard, thirsty work. If ever a rabbit deserved a drink, he deserved one now.

"Come on, Eightsy!" Three-Twenty-Three scampered past him. "The first match is about to start!"

He put the gourd down, and lolloped after his brother. Maybe he'd feel like a drink tomorrow, and maybe he wouldn't. Maybe he'd party all night and maybe he'd stay in. There was room in his life for both.

And for sunsets. Always for sunsets.

3

CASE STUDY

Hypothesis

At the Velogalactic Company Limited (head office: Pluto), we constantly strive to understand and support the needs of our valued customers and potential customers.

As Sales Manager, Outlying Minor Planets Division, I agreed to visit Planet K-137 and investigate, in the words of my line manager, "why the bloody cats aren't buying the bloody bikes".

K-137 is a horticultural planet, producing flowers and bulbs for interplanetary trade. The flower fields are irrigated by a network of canals.

The installed species is feline in form, created using genetic material from a number of small cats in the genus *Felis*, including the black-footed cat and the jungle or swamp cat. Referred to by traders as 'tigerlilies', they were introduced to tend the flowers and control the various species of bird and rodent either native to the planet or inadvertently imported by visiting aliens.

Bipedal, they stand approximately one metre tall, with an average weight of around 30kg in Earth gravity. Males tend to be larger and heavier. The fur may be either a solid grey or rust colour, or tawny with small spots. The ears are rounded. The pads of the paws, and surrounding fur, are black. A tail is present, as it is in many created species. Although no longer necessary for balance, it is simpler to leave the tail in place than to edit it out, and tails are also perceived as aesthetically pleasing.

The cats are solitary, with each individual patrolling a large territory. Their diet consists mainly of rodents and birds, supplemented by fish and frogs from the canals.

The flowers of K-137 are classed as a luxury item and grown under strictly controlled conditions. The use of pesticides is banned. Larger vermin are kept in check by the cats, and insect pests by predator species such as spiders and ladybirds. The flowers are pollinated by bees; looking after the beehives is another task assigned to the cats.

Solar or wind power, or hydroelectricity, is used, to prevent pollution of the flower fields. Spaceships orbit K-137's moon with their engines powered off, and are loaded using water-powered elevators. Harvesting, the spreading of natural fertilisers and other tasks are carried out by hand rather than using machinery, to enhance the luxury experience. Once harvested, the flowers are placed in sub-zero suspension for space travel—arriving, according to the current advertising campaign, "as fresh as the instant they were picked by kitten paws".

The environmental legislation of the planet, combined with the need of the cats to travel long distances as they carry out their work, would seem to make the inhabitants of K-137 ideal customers for the products of the Velogalactic Bicycle Company Limited (head office: Pluto).

However, sales proved sluggish, and I was determined to drive them up.

Method

I met Rush, my host, at her home in K-137's upper northern sector. She is 25 standard years of age, with reddish fur.

Insofar as the cats have a structured society, Rush is a local figure of some importance. As an area supervisor, she is responsible for ensuring that harvest quotas and quality standards are met; a role not dissimilar, perhaps, to a Sales Manager. I hoped that if I persuaded her to purchase one of our products, others would follow suit.

Rush welcomed me and we sat down to a meal of fish stew. (Since cats obtain all the nutrients they need from meat and fish, I took supplements during my stay to counteract the lack of grains and vegetables in my diet.)

I noticed there was little furniture in Rush's home. We dined sitting on mats woven from reeds, and later we would sleep on them.

In the night, I woke to find Rush draping a blanket over me.

"I forgot you don't have fur," she said.

The next morning, I introduced Rush to the Velogalactic Company Limited's latest model, the Photon. Combining an ultralight frame with convenient folding technology and all-terrain wheels, it is an excellent performer both on and off road. Our sales brochure describes it as 'a joy to ride' and 'built for both comfort and speed'. Our salespeople, unofficially, describe it as 'sex on wheels'.

Rush had never ridden a bicycle before, but her feline sense of balance is acute, so she did not require much teaching. We set off along one of the canalside paths to inspect the territory she covers. I was riding my own bike, an original Venus racer. (Although the company encourages us to upgrade at a deep discount, I like the Venus and I have made a number of modifications to it over the years.)

The lack of atmospheric pollution makes the sunlight on K-

137 exceptionally pure and strong. The water glittered, and, to our right, fields of red and yellow flowers stretched to the horizon. In front of me, Rush cycled steadily, the sun turning her russet fur to gold and tracing a bright line around each hair.

The first problem became apparent almost immediately. Rush's tail, which swayed from side to side as she pedalled, came so dangerously close to getting trapped in the spokes of the rear wheel that I drew up alongside her and yelled at her to stop. She dismounted, ears flat and fur bristling, and I explained the issue.

I was able to improvise a guard for the rear wheel using a flattened drinks container and some wire. It spoiled the lines of the Photon rather, but that seemed preferable to spoiling the lines of Rush.

We continued our ride, past windmills that cast whirling shadows on the flower fields. Sometimes we stopped so Rush could inspect the plants for signs of rodent infestation. I joined her as she walked through the lines of flowers, brushing against them; feline scent discourages pests. Pollen and petals decorated my clothes and her fur as we passed, and the foliage rippled with the wind or the passage of fleeing wildlife.

Towards the end of the morning, I noticed that Rush was tiring faster than I had anticipated. I pedalled alongside her so I could analyse her riding style.

A cat's forelimbs are almost as long as the hind, enabling them to travel on all fours when necessary or convenient. This meant that the handlebars and pedals were not in the optimum position for Rush to power the machine. I adjusted the handlebar height as far as I could, but it was still less than ideal. Furthermore, cats walk in digitigrade stance, like a human on tiptoe. Rush's hind paws did not fit the bicycle's toeclips, causing wasted effort on the upstroke of each cycle. This was something I wouldn't be able to fix with the portable toolkit I'd brought on the ride, but would have to wait for our return.

While I worked, Rush caught two fish in the traditional manner: by scooping them out of the canal with her paw. She killed and gutted them, and strung them on a pole for transport. This we attached to the rear carrier.

When the sun was at its highest point, we stopped for lunch. We chose a spot by a bridge, where Rush could sprawl out in the sun while I sheltered in the shade.

She cooked the fish in a solar-powered boiler. I suggested a barbecue, but that would fall foul of K-137's pollution laws.

"Well?" I asked. "What do you think?"

A tour of inspection that would ordinarily have taken all day had been completed in a couple of hours. I expected to find Rush full of praise for the Photon.

She twisted her head to lick a tuft of fur on her shoulder back into place, turned back and stared intently at me, her green eyes slightly crossed and the pupils narrow in the sunlight.

"Chris...tine," she said, struggling to push the syllables through her carnivore's teeth. "Why do the bikes have to be adapted for us? Why can't they be built for us in the first place?"

Please consider this my letter of resignation from the Velogalactic Company Limited (head office: Pluto).

I am happy to work my one month's notice period, or to take 28 days' paid gardening leave in accordance with company policy, before starting my new career as joint CEO of Rush Bikes Unlimited.

I undertake not to encroach on Velogalactic sales territory, nor to use information or contacts gained during my employment against my former employer.

I have learned many valuable lessons from my time as Sales Manager, Outlying Minor Planets Division, and I plan to use these going forward as we create a client-centric organisation using a bottom-up approach.

Not everyone in the galaxy is humanoid in form, and rather than offering a one size fits all solution, we will recognise and celebrate the fact by designing from scratch for each and every life form.

You have your client base. We have ours. And ours offers infinite possibilities.

4

THE LION OF THE LOW COUNTRIES

"There you go, Mr Belgicus. One latte and one waffle with cream and Nutella."

Leo thanked the waitress and sipped his coffee, staring out across the cobbled square with its soothing splash of fountains. The morning sunlight shrank his pupils and played on the faded words that spotted his coat. He stretched out an arm, claws extended, and turned it over to feel the warmth on the unlettered inside of his wrist.

Even in the rarefied world of heraldry, Leo Belgicus was an oddball. Back in the early days of the Renaissance, some artistic cartographer had noticed that the borders of the then Low Countries formed a shape that somewhat resembled a lion rampant, and a symbol had been born. He was proud of the fine details that mapped his skin, the rivers and villages, but they rewarded close and careful browsing. From afar, he was a mess. While other national creatures in bold, simple shapes were raised aloft on their countries' flags, he was stuck in a book. Maybe that was why they all seemed to look down on him.

He flipped his tablet open and created a new document.

LIONS   INTERNATIONAL   CONFERENCE: KEYNOTE

SPEECH, he typed, then, exhausted by this burst of creativity, took a bite of his waffle. Licking cream from his nose, he considered his next line.

Relevance, that was the key. He needed to fit in to this modern age, but it wasn't easy. The *zeitgeist* rushed along like a Eurostar train. Miss, and you bellyflop onto the tracks, left behind in a cloud of embarrassment. Back in the Nineties, his PR officer had got Leo to perform a rap on national television. The memory still made his ink run cold, and even eating the PR officer had been a poor consolation.

The conference used to be a highlight of his year. Now, he was dreading it. Young tyros like Lev Two-Tails, the silver lion of Czechia, already treated him with open contempt. 'Paper lion', Lev had called him at the last one. "You know, like a paper tiger. Because you are maps? Ha!"

He switched to his newsfeed and browsed the headlines. Terrorism. Unemployment. Political extremists. Refugees crowding in from places where things were far worse. The general feeling seemed to be that the whole world was unravelling; was it any wonder that nobody had time for Leo?

As a national animal, Leo's purpose was to kindle his people's pride in their country by reminding them of their history. Once, just stalking regally through the streets had been enough; now he stopped passers-by for conversation, like some religious fanatic or double glazing salesperson. More and more often, he either heard that history was boring and stuffy, or that the past was full of dubious conquests and prejudices of which he should be ashamed.

Be strong, he willed the people crossing the square. *Be brave. Remember your past. We've come through worse than this.*

A girl holding a teddy bear looked his way, briefly. Nobody else spared him a glance. All wrapped up in their mobile phones as usual. Above them, the flags of the EU and Belgium waved. Stars and stripes. Huh.

Leo examined himself in the metal surface of the table. He was a lion! A funny-shaped lion, but instantly recognisable nonetheless. He was noble and fierce! He represented the proud spirit of his people! He… should probably cut down on the waffles.

Leo had always been on the short and chunky side, his shape dictated by the old national borders, but there was no excuse for the way his tummy bulged out at present. If anything, he should be losing weight, the way his map had changed. Wars and treaties had nicked an ear here, taken a chunk from his tail there, scarred his sides and ripped hanks from his mane. The states and towns that labelled him were blurring as their names faded from public memory. Once, they had stood out brightly, tattoos that rippled with his muscles. Now he looked like some neglected piece of public sculpture, chipped and scribbled on by bored teenagers.

Across the square, a tourist pointed her camera. Leo smiled, toothily, and raised his paw in a regal wave. Not everyone recognised him these days, even his own people. Like the ancient placenames on his maps, he was fading from their memory. He wasn't available on postcards, or as a plastic figurine. On the merchandise front, he'd lost out to a statue of a small boy piddling.

He closed the news down and logged in to LION, the Lions International Online Network. Only the venerable lion of the United Kingdom was showing as available, which was fine with Leo; insofar as he had friends, the British Lion was his best one. He sent a private chat request. After a few seconds a video window popped open, showing the familiar grave and golden face.

Leo narrowed his eyes respectfully. You don't mess with Lyonesse.

"Hullo, LB. Looks like a nice morning over there. Filthy in London as usual. How's the keynote going?"

"Morning, Nessie. Actually, I'm a bit worried about it. I'm having a hard time finding something to say that's relevant, you know?"

Like Leo, the British Lion had seen her empire dwindle over the centuries as other nations rose to power. There were certain subjects you didn't bring up with Lyonesse, like the loss of America, and why she had a mane (sexual dimorphism wasn't a concept with which artists in the Dark Ages were greatly familiar, and most of them painted with the vague idea that a lion was a large, gold cat in a wig), but her dignity and seniority were such that nobody dared give her a hard time.

"Pff. What do you mean, 'relevant'? Edgy? On trend? Radical, perhaps?" Lyonesse had never let him forget his foray into rap. He felt his territories flush red. "You're better than that, Leo. Pay no attention to those... those hipster neckmanes."

"They're right, though. Nobody reads my blog. I applied to sponsor a brand of chip sauce and got turned down." He gulped, and made his most damning confession. "It wasn't even the leading brand."

"Dear me. Tintin and Poirot still ignoring your dinner invitations, too?" The onscreen face of Lyonesse smirked. "I have faith in you, LB. I know your speech is going to put Belgium on the map again."

Leo nodded acknowledgement of the old joke, though his tail, unseen under the table, twitched with annoyance.

"I just feel...a bit unwanted," he muttered into his mane.

"Nonsense! Everyone's always happy to see you, mapface. Are you bringing some of those caramel biscuity things?"

"*Stroopwafels*," Leo supplied, sadly. "Well, talk to you soon."

He closed the window. There it was: to his peers, Leo Belgicus, the Lion of the Low Countries, was nothing but a supplier of Belgian treats. A portly, cuddly joke.

And to the people of Belgium, a virtual unknown. Nobody cared about the past any more; they just wanted the future.

Music and cartoons from the USA and Japan. Yet, at the same time, they were scared and unhappy. The prevailing view, he gathered, was that while they welcomed new things into the country on their own terms, the new people who came here looking for work or safety were less welcome. They would take all the jobs, or refuse jobs and take money from the state (nobody seemed entirely clear on this point) and they would dilute the national identity.

But part of your identity is sitting right here! He wanted to jump up on the seat of the artsy steel café chair that was currently making his backside cold and sore, and roar it out. But would any of them hear?

Maybe it was time to head home. Work on his stupid speech in peace. Some decades ago, Leo had established himself in the Atomium, the huge, futuristic metal sculpture built for the 1958 World's Fair in Brussels. Already it was hopelessly dated, but in this case it somehow didn't matter because it was retro. Fashions changed so quickly now. Times past, a castle was good for several centuries if you hung up a new tapestry every so often.

There was a tram stop somewhere around here, but to his annoyance he wasn't quite sure of the direction. He beckoned the waitress.

"Seven Euro, please, Mr Belgicus." She spoke Flemish with a slight accent from somewhere to the east.

The stipend Leo had been granted by the state predated both the franc and the liard, rendering it worthless in today's money, and his image was long out of copyright, so he didn't receive royalties. It was lucky he'd invested in gold and diamonds, which he converted whenever the rate was favourable.

He drew out his wallet, then paused.

"You...weren't born in Belgium, were you?" he asked, trying not to offend. "But you recognised me. How's that?"

"You're part of the citizenship course!" She smiled. "I've

forgotten a lot of what I learned, but I remember you. Your face looked so friendly."

He was supposed to look fierce, but Leo found he didn't mind. He smiled back. Reaching in his wallet again, he picked out a mid-sized diamond.

"Thank you, but I can't accept this."

"I won't tell your boss."

"It's not that. I had to study the whole history of Belgium, you know. The bad bits too. I can guess why you have diamonds."

Leo dropped his gaze. "Do you know how to get to Labrador Road?" he asked.

She frowned. "Let's see, you need to head for…er…"

"Can you show me on here?" He flexed a bicep so the town plan stood out. Brussels on his muscles. That had been a good pickup line, in the past, but the waitress just shook her head.

"I don't recognise any of these places. Don't you have a maps app?"

"A maps app? Why would *I* need a maps app?" He shrugged indignantly, displaying the towns and geographical features across his chest.

"Why are you *lost?*" The waitress leaned across him and tapped at the screen of his tablet. "There!"

With a series of gestures too intricate and precise for lion paws, she brought up a plan of the city and zoomed in on the red blob that marked their location.

"There. Head up that street and turn left at McDonald's…sir? Mr Belgicus? Are you all right?" She waved a hand in front of his nose.

The Lion of the Low Countries stared straight ahead, a new light dancing in his parchment-coloured eyes.

———

Leo tapped triumphantly at a laptop key. On the screen above his head, the familiar portrait of Leo Belgicus appeared: the side view, with one forepaw raised, head high, and a long, red tongue lolling out. When he zoomed in on Dunkirk, at the base of his tail, a street plan appeared. A button changed the view, so Leo and his audience could see a reconstruction of the town as it had been in the Renaissance, and a scrollbar moved the map back and forth through the centuries.

The team from the software company had spent weeks photographing and scanning Leo from every angle. He'd seen parts of himself he hadn't known existed, and resolved to groom more thoroughly in future. High resolution imagery was not kind to centuries-old fur or whiskery chins, and the border hamlets between his toes deserved to be presented in their best light.

He had helped them with the modelling of each town through the ages, too; after all, he had been there. Now he could revisit and share a past nobody else alive remembered. It was incredible, this skipping about in history.

Aware that he had spent rather too long engrossed in a graphical representation of his own bottom, Leo raised his eyes.

"Historians can use it," he said, "and fiction writers. Children in school, too. And the new people coming in, the immigrants, they can learn about their new country. But it's fun for everyone. Give it a try when you get home!" The URL flashed up on the screen.

The audience of national lions made polite noises of appreciation. Someone, probably Lyonesse, began to clap, but when nobody else joined in, the noise faltered and stopped. They were intrigued, though; Leo could tell by the tilted heads and the ears turned towards the podium.

It had been fun, working with the programmers, and flattering to hold their attention, even if they were mostly intrigued by the challenges of rendering him in pixels, or whatever they were called. What had really excited Leo, though, was the sensation of being a symbol to them. As, once, he had provided something to rally round and fight for, so his very shape and form spurred the maps team on to new feats of programming.

There were other things, too, that he was keeping to himself for now. His visits to the borders to welcome newcomers into Belgium, and the care packages he funded by selling off his stores of treasure from the bad colonial days.

"Any questions?" he said, into the hush.

Lev Two-Tails raised a silver paw. "We all know something that looks cool today can be hideously out of place in a few decades," he said. "How do you know this won't be one of them?"

"Are you referring to my brief career as a rap star?" Leo asked, before anyone else could.

"Actually, I was thinking of Communism," said the younger lion. "But the point still stands."

"*My* point," Leo replied, "is that it doesn't matter if something we try turns out to be silly, as long as we keep trying."

"Isn't that just delaying the inevitable? All this effort, just to keep up appearances. If they don't need us any more, and we can't help them, maybe we should just…fade away."

Leo, startled, looked properly at Lyonesse; noticed how old and tired she looked. As his gaze wandered across the assembled lions, with their fur of *argent* and *gules* and *or*, he realised that he wasn't the only one who felt left behind as the decades moved on. Even Lev had seen his territory chopped and changed over a relatively short lifespan. Many of them, like him, had watched the blue flag with its gold stars creep into their territory, and wondered what it heralded.

"We've all been afraid of change," Leo told them. "Our countries change, our people change, and we worry they'll reject us. They make new alliances and unions, and we get scared that they won't need us any more. They form bigger and bigger societies, and we're afraid they'll lose their identity, and us."

He spread his paws, widening the gaps between neighbouring hamlets.

"But look at us! Look at LION! I can get hold of any of you for a chat, whenever I want. Lev can show me what's going on in his country, just using his phone. And in a few years, all this will sound just as quaint as telex."

"Telex the thing? Or Telex the synthpop band?"

"Lev," Lyonesse warned, and the Czech lion subsided, swishing his two tails. Leo plunged onward.

"When our people disperse to other countries, they need things that remind them of home. Food. Comic books. Flags. The very things that the new ones who come in adopt to help them learn and fit in. When online friends say, 'hey, what's it like living in Belgium, or Czechia, or wherever'—we're part of that. We're Lions *International*, remember?"

He was freestyling now, going off the map. It was a heady feeling. Leo tossed his head back and shook out his mane.

"There might not be flags where we're going," he said. "There might not be borders, or nations. But there will be lions. And there will definitely be *stroopwafels*."

He left the stage to furious applause. Even though some of it might have been at the prospect of biscuits, he was confident that some was for his speech. He hoped he was right about the future, but it wasn't his place to try and influence it. He just brought the past to the table, for his people to remember the good bits and acknowledge the bad bits. He had rallied the lions and he would rally his nation, too. He'd like to see a pissing statue arouse such passion in its audience!

The other delegates stood, beginning to mingle and head for the refreshments. The low purr of their chatter had a cheerful, excited tone.

As Leo made his way past Lyonesse, she put a paw on his shoulder and touched her warm, pink nose against his inky one.

"Excellent speech, LB," she growled into his ear, her beard tickling the sensitive hairs there.

He rustled at her touch, and for the second time that morning he looked at the old British lion as if he had never seen her before.

Somewhere inside Leo Belgicus, a border crumbled.

5

SUBNIVEAL

He was called Lem. All lemmings are.

From the time they left their mothers until in due course they died, his species lived fierce, solitary little lives. A nod of acknowledgement and a gruff "Lem" as they squeezed past each other in the tunnels sufficed, or an "Oh, Lem!" for the occasions, a few in a lifetime, when two lemmings courted.

His brothers and sister were Lem, too, but his mother, for now, was Mother, who kept him warm, fed him milk, and told him stories. Lem was a sightless pink baby, and Mother's squeaks at first were meaningless noise that soothed him to sleep, but it was not long before they formed words: thrilling tales of a world beyond the soft warmth of the nest.

"Pause and listen," she told her litter. "While you hunt for food, pause and listen for the paws of the Snow-walkers above your head, and freeze when you hear them, or you will be seized from the snowpack and plucked out into the Cold Open as a meal. Eat grass and grow fat while the Long Dark lasts, but beware the Snow-walkers: the Tunnel-creep with his long and slender body who glides death through our very homes; the Grab-claws who floats above the snow on silent wings, and strikes without warning. Beware the Day-bringer above all, the great snow fox who pounces on our rustling and brings the tunnels crashing down."

Lem shuddered and snuggled himself closer to his sister Lem and brothers Lem. Mother licked his stomach to stimulate the muscles that turned her milk into energy so Lem could grow.

"The Day-bringer smashes down on Lem's tunnels, so the bright light and the cold rush in, and grabs Lem while Lem blinks and shivers in confusion. Beware the Day-bringer who swallows the sun at summer's end, so that she might stalk Lem in the Long Dark."

By the time he was a week old, with a soft coat of new hair on his belly, Lem knew the story by heart. At this point he blurted, "But Lem was too clever for her!"

"That's right, Lem," his mother said, giving him her teat to hush him while she continued. "We sank down below the deep snow, where holes and tunnels form. The tunnels give us warmth and shelter, they keep our food from frost, and they shield us from the Snow-walkers. We criss and cross through the Long Dark, and rarely does Lem meet Lem. When we do meet, we hiss and chatter our teeth."

"And then!" Lem squeaked with his mouth full of milk.

"Ssh, Lem." She curled herself around her five babies. "And then the Day-bringer brings forth the day again. She grows sleepy and yawns, and the sun peeps out. Each day she yawns a little wider, and the sun stays out for longer. The tunnel walls grow wet and thin, and collapse on themselves. No shelter now from the Snow-walkers, and Lem meets Lem more often in the Cold Open. When all the Cold Open is buzzing with us, we can bear it no longer, and we must run for the Low Land."

"Where is the Low Land?" Lem asked. His brothers and sister were asleep, but Lem was wide awake, pressing his paws against his mother's flank.

"I have not seen it, little Lem, because I was born under the snow, like you. They say it is many days' travel away, and dangerous voyaging. Many of us will die on the journey."

"And when will the Day-bringer bring the day?"

"I don't know. Soon."

"Can't we stop it?"

"Some things cannot be stopped, Lem."

"I don't want to die in the Cold Open."

"You may not die. But, then again, you may. It won't matter very much. Enough of us will live that Lem will go on and on forever. That, too, is a thing that cannot be stopped. Now go to sleep!"

Lem could not close his eyes, because they had not yet opened. Nor could he go to sleep for a long time, minutes and minutes. There were things that could not be stopped. And there was something in the world that his mother didn't know, and couldn't protect him from.

When his eyes did open, there was little to see. His big, warm mother had a rounded shape. His sister and brothers were Mother in miniature. In the gloom, he made out their faces by the pale yellow cheeks and black markings. The nesting-space in which they lived was stuffed with grass and the soft under-wool of musk ox. Lem buried his nose in it and sniffed, trying to imagine the Cold Open where the great beasts walked. He crawled to the mouth of the den, but his new eyes could see nothing beyond it. Without the bodies of his family around him, he grew cold quickly. Mother fetched him back and tucked him in beside her.

The next time he tried, his legs were stronger, and his mother seemed less fussed about retrieving him. She was giving him less milk, and he felt, too, as if he wanted something more than milk. He had new little teeth, and he ground them together.

The third time he reached the den mouth, he kept going.

The tunnels were dim and blue around him, with dark flecks where dirt and debris were encased in the snow. In some places, the passages were tight around his shoulders; elsewhere they arched far above his head. Under the snow, the grass grew thin and sour, but plentiful enough to power his legs and keep his brain moving.

Sometimes he bumped into other lemmings in the passages, if he smelled and heard them too late to take a different turning, and he greeted them with gnashing teeth.

Our Lem might have been handsome by lemming standards, with large and liquid eyes, fur marbled with black, cream and yellow like a pebble underwater, and a diagonal black stripe across his face. He might also have been an ugly lemming. Nobody ever told him either way.

Soon Lem had been away from his mother for more sleeps than he knew how to count. He had eaten such a great quantity of seeds and grasses that he had almost forgotten the taste of milk, and he would not have known his mother or his four littermates if they had met in the tunnels. He remembered the stories, but he had forgotten the scents.

There were more streaks and lumps of matter in the roof and walls, which dripped with water now. New holes appeared, large enough to swallow his paw and, later, his head.

The time arrived when he met another lemming in the tunnels and saw the glitter in her eyes and the white shine of her teeth; the rakish cap of black fur on her head and the waves of yellow along her flanks.

Light. It was getting light.

The Day-bringer was coming.

"Lem," he grunted, moving aside to let the other pass.

"Lem to you, too," she replied. The soft tangle of her fur brushed his hip, pushing his other side against the tunnel wall. The snow gave a little, and its cold dampness seeped into his skin to make him shiver.

A new scent pricked his nose, strong and rank and bloody, and he pulled his lips back from his teeth. He heard the slither of a long body and the scraping of long claws. The head of a creature emerged, dirty yellow in the blue light, more pointed than Lem's blunt little snout. Lem knew he was looking into the face of a Tunnel-creep.

He opened his mouth and squalled at it, a sound that echoed and bounced from the ice walls and would tell other lemmings to scatter and hide. The Tunnel-creep flattened its ears and hesitated. Lem breathed in so his body puffed up, and shrieked again.

Behind him, the other lemming chattered. She leaped for a smaller tunnel that branched from the main thoroughfare. Her feet and stubby tail wriggled as she shoved her way in, and yelling Lem, even in his terror, reflected that her hindquarters looked nice.

The Tunnel-creep lunged forward. Lem smelled its meaty breath, and saw himself reflected in black eyes.

Like the female, Lem was still young and small. He jumped backwards from the sharp teeth and the eyes, and popped into the side tunnel bottom first. The muzzle of the Tunnel-creep plunged after him, filling the entrance hole and bringing darkness. Teeth snapped at his nose. Lem squeaked and squirmed backwards.

The heat of his fear and motion in the enclosed space was stifling. His claws gouged new marks in the floor, and a long-buried root scraped a deep scratch along his flank. The roof brushed his ears as he crawled, still staring at the Tunnel-creep. It scraped and scrabbled, but could not follow its snout through the gap. The sharp teeth snapped for a while, then the ermine withdrew its muzzle. The smell faded and the strange new light returned. The tunnel widened just enough for Lem to turn himself around, his fur sticking up in all directions.

The other lemming looked back to make sure he was safe,

then scurried off without a word. Lem watched until the shadows hid her.

The light faded from the tunnels. He pretended it had never been there, but it was back after his next sleep, and this time it stayed longer.

The world he had always known was slipping away. Soon it would be gone completely, leaving him exposed to the huge rawness of the Cold Open. Now he noticed the passing of each day by the light shining through the tunnels, and with every day, the light lingered later and shone brighter. The tunnels were wider and wetter, with new holes through which the wind brought new smells. There seemed to be more lemmings in the tunnels every day—growing bigger, moving faster, eating more, jostling and chattering more fiercely.

Yet, of them all, our Lem was the one to have the idea.

His mother had told him that the only way to beat the Snow-walkers was by hiding, but hadn't he scared the Tunnel-creep, then outwitted and outrun it? So then. Lem must go forth and slay the Day-bringer.

Thus he would stop the world from melting and save Lem from their long journey to the Low Land.

He had set himself a difficult task. The Day-bringer was the size of twenty lemmings, and could devour that many in a day. She walked softly on broad feet, listening all the time with her pointed ears for the rustle of the lemmings below. Lem would need his wits, and he would need a weapon. His teeth and voice had been enough to drive a Tunnel-creep back, but the Day-bringer was larger, and he wanted to kill, not just hold off.

The twigs and grass stems buried in the tunnel walls were no good; they were brittle and broke in his paws. His own teeth and claws were too small to get through the dense fur of the Day-bringer.

Then, as he wandered the passages, he found his way blocked by a thin shaft of ice that dripped from the roof to the floor. He tried to bite through the root, but its coldness hurt his teeth, so he snapped it off by throwing his body against it. To grip it hurt his paws, so he wrapped the thicker end in moss. He was ready to begin his search.

He moved through the more remote tunnels, because, solitary though he was, he had no wish to bring death down on any other lemmings. Besides, the quieter it was in the tunnels, the better he could hear Snow-walkers above his head. He paused and listened. Once he moved towards a rustling sound, only to realise that it came from within the tunnel itself. He backed away as quickly and quietly as he could from the harsh, dangerous scent of the Tunnel-creep and chose a different route. Tunnel-creeps didn't swallow the day and bring it forth again, so they were useless to him.

The walls of his world were shiny and dripping. The floor was almost all wet grass now; where the snow remained, his paws sank deep into it and came out damp. Lem squelched along, gripping his stick of ice. At night he wrapped it in musk-ox wool so it would not stick to the tunnel while he slept, and to slow its melting.

Sometimes he passed a place where the roof had caved in, or a lemming had pushed through it. From the claw marks in the snow, lemmings were already running out into the Cold Open. All Lem had to do was poke his head up, and he would see it for himself. But the tunnels were all he had ever known, and beyond lay vast, dangerous cold. He pushed on beneath the snow. His spear of ice grew more slender all the time, and his chances with it. One more sleep, he told himself, and then he would go into the world above to hunt the Day-bringer on her own grounds.

But the Day-bringer came to him.

She came in a shower of falling snow, a flash of light, and a rush of warm, hard muscle. The world fell in on him, and he felt the full power of the sun on his skin for the first time. The wind whipped at his fur, and the light made him squeeze his eyes shut. When he forced them open, he was pinned on his back beneath the paw of what seemed, in the glare, to be a glowing ball of white light. He did not doubt for an instant that this was the creature which had swallowed the sun and was now bringing it forth, yawn by yawn. He raised his spear of ice and jabbed it as hard as he could at the Day-bringer's chest.

It met the soft resistance of her thick fur and slipped from his paws.

"What are you doing, prey?" she snarled.

The first thing Lem noticed was that her mouth was pink, not white and bright with the power of the sun inside her.

The second was the sharpness of her many teeth.

"I've come to slay you," he squeaked. "To stop you yawning and bringing forth the sun."

"I do what?" She blinked and relaxed her paw a little, though not enough to let Lem wriggle free.

"The Day-bringer swallows the sun and makes the Long Dark," Lem explained. "If I kill you, the sun won't come back and the snow will stay hard. I won't have to go out into the Cold Open, and maybe lose my life trying to find my way to the Low Land."

He squinted at the great snow fox. She was huge to his eyes, but he found it doubtful that she could have swallowed something capable of lighting the whole world. Had he been caught by the wrong Day-bringer?

"Silly little prey! Some things cannot be stopped. I cannot keep the spring from coming, any more than I can keep my white coat from turning brown. But when it does, I shall hunt lemming on grass as easily as I did in the winter snow. The changing seasons look after a fox, as they would have looked after you. Now I am going to eat you. And that, too, is a thing that cannot be stopped."

With that, she picked him up in her teeth and tossed him

into the air, so that she might snap his back in her jaws when she caught him. Lem spun, his feet paddling. As he rose he saw the Cold Open, white streaked with grey and brown; the sparkling rush of moving water beyond, and far in the distance, the lush green of the Low Land. He even saw the sun, its pale springtime face awesome to his winter eyes, and most definitely shining in the sky rather than imprisoned behind the Day-bringer's teeth. Lem was sorry that he had lived all his life in the tunnels, only to have it ended by the Day-bringer before he could go on his great journey. He reached the top of his arc and fell back towards the streaked snow on his unstoppable voyage into the waiting white jaws.

And a white shape swooped down towards him out of the low sun, wings beating swiftly and silently, in pursuit of this airborne morsel of lemming.

Lem, in the air, made himself flat. Talons raked the fur of his back as the Grab-claws missed its mark. Lem reached with his paws and caught tail feathers.

The arctic fox leaped, and collided in her leap with the snowy owl as it swung off balance.

Lem tumbled to the ground—lay winded for a moment—pelted away across the Cold Open in a zigzag run.

"Then I will eat *you!*" Snow-walker screamed at Grab-claws, plucking feathers with her teeth as the great bird flapped and pecked.

By the time the two predators had separated, one staggering into the sky and the other licking a cut paw, neither of them could spot the lemming in the vastness of the Cold Open. Lem's mottled coat blended in with both the winter's snow and the bare brown grass of the autumn before he was born. His spear of ice, forgotten, lay melting in the spring sun.

Some things could be stopped after all.

The journey Lem must make to the Low Land, of course, had only just begun. He made the voyage over days and weeks, sometimes on his own, sometimes jostled by other lemmings. He swam rivers and dodged the Day-bringers in their brown summer fur. Many died on the way, as Lem's mother had told him: eaten by the Snow-walkers, drowned in the rivers. It would not have been important to the species of lemmings as a whole if our Lem had died, but it was important to him, and he lived.

The Low Land was not the end of his travels, nor was it entirely safe; there were still Day-bringers and Grab-claws to evade, and Tunnel-creeps too, although now they hid in the bushes instead of creeping through tunnels. But it is a good place to leave our Lem. There was plenty of food, and even the company of other lemmings didn't seem so bad any more. Before too long, there was one lemming who made him say "Oh, Lem!", and who said "Oh, Lem!" to him in return.

It would be nice to think she was the lemming he met beneath the snow on the day of the Tunnel-creep, when his first sight of another's face and fur made him realise the sun was coming. Perhaps she was. All lemmings are called Lem, after all.

6

THE PHILOSOPHER AND THE WEASEL

Socrates was sitting cross-legged in his cell when the weasel bellied in through a gap at the base of the wall.

It was a beautiful little beast, bright-eyed, with soft, russet fur fading to cream on its stomach. The slender tail, tufted at the end, bobbed up and down as the weasel travelled across the floor with a liquid, looping motion. To Socrates, it seemed such a perfect creation that it might have been the original Form or Idea of a weasel on which all other weasels were modelled. The philosopher sat still as a marble statue, watching his visitor sniff and scurry its way to the uneaten crust in his clay bowl.

"*Kaire*, Big Beard!" said the weasel. "Mind if I take this?"

The philosopher put a hand to his chin. "There are two possibilities here," he said aloud to himself—but softly, so as not to frighten the animal. "Either this weasel is talking, or I am imagining it due to hunger, loneliness or madness. I do not consider that I am mad, for I can still reason, and I have been hungry and alone before, yet nothing of this sort has happened. Besides, if this were a trick played by my mind to keep me company, why a weasel?"

The weasel cocked its head and stared up at him. "You could be dreaming," it offered.

"True, little friend, but in dreams a stone floor never felt this cold and hard, nor have I ever wondered in my dreams if I was dreaming. No, you are a talking weasel, and I ask myself if you are a god in disguise, if you alone among weasels can speak, or if all weasels can speak but none has until now spoken to me."

"I don't think I'm a god," said the weasel, though from the way it preened, the idea was clearly pleasing, "because the gods don't require mortal food, and right now I require that bread." It eyed the crust again.

"You can not only talk, but reason!" Socrates marvelled. "Why do you want the bread?"

"Because I want to live," replied the weasel. "Why are you locked up in here?" it added, standing up on its hind legs to get a better look at the bearded man.

"Because I also want to live."

"Are you hiding from your enemies, then?" It puffed out its fur, ready to defend itself—and maybe Socrates too—if enemies burst in.

"No—in fact, my enemies put me here."

"And they'll let you out soon?"

Socrates gave the upward nod that meant a negative. "They are going to kill me, because they say I have blasphemed against the gods and led the youth of Athens astray. They would let me go if I renounced the things I have said, but I will not, and tomorrow they will bring me hemlock to drink. The bread is safe, though," he added.

The weasel's front paws shifted up and down on the edge of the bowl, its nose a thumb's breadth from the crust. But it couldn't resist another question.

"So you'll die if you stay? You said you wanted to live!"

"Weasel—what does it mean to be alive?"

"Eh?"

"I am alive. You are alive. The bowl and the crust are not. What do living things like us have in common?"

"Eating!" the weasel said brightly. "If I don't eat, I die. I move so quickly and my heart beats so fast that I need to spend pretty much all my time hunting and eating to stay warm and alive." Its acorn-shaped head darted forwards and it snapped up the crust, which hung from its mouth like a brown beard. Socrates uncrossed his legs and leaned against the wall, watching his guest.

"It's true that you eat and I eat, but does not fire also consume? Is fire alive, then?"

"Ungh." The weasel dropped most of the bread to the floor, chewed its mouthful thoughtfully and swallowed before replying. "No...no, it's not." It poked the remains with a tiny claw.

"Oh, don't stop eating, please!" said Socrates. "It may not be the characteristic that makes you alive, but it is still necessary! Think about what you said just now."

The weasel looked down at itself. "I'm warm...and I move about,"—it demonstrated, scampering in a little circle—"and my heart beats. The dead are still and cold."

"True again. But consider plants. Are plants alive?"

"Yes!" cried the weasel, pacing up and down. "But they don't have hearts and they don't move!"

"They move a little. Yet even a dead tree may sway in the wind. Try again!" Socrates leaned gently forwards and extended a finger to the weasel.

"Growing! Plants grow bigger and so do animals!" It touched its nose to the philosopher's hand and darted away again.

"Children grow, yes, but old men such as myself, we shrink. We are still alive, though, are we not?" He cupped his hand coaxingly. The weasel moved towards him with a sideways motion, brushed his hand with its cheek, then climbed into his palm. Socrates held it against his chest.

"You're alive. And warm!" It pressed itself to him. Socrates could feel the quick heartbeat, like a fluttering leaf.

"What about puddles?" the philosopher continued.

"Puddles?" The little head cocked, puzzled.

"Puddles grow in the rain, and so do rivers and the other bodies of water. And fire, again—fire grows larger as it feeds."

"O, Big Beard!" wailed the weasel. "You've got me so confused I don't know if I'm alive or not!" It gave his thumb a little nip.

Socrates stroked its head with his forefinger. "Don't doubt that you are alive, weasel. You're quick with life, fizzing with it —this old man delights to see such a vigorous creature." He rubbed at the soft fur under its chin. "To say you're not alive would be like saying you're not a colour, when you're red as a fox and white as snow on Mount Olympus. Yet if I were to ask, 'what is colour?', you might find that question difficult too. It is a problem I have spoken of in the past. At present we are discussing life—at the end of mine."

The weasel was silent for a few moments. Its eyes were closed and its nose pointed at the ceiling as Socrates rubbed its chest and belly.

"Tell me something," Socrates said at last. "My kind think that your kind, the weasels, conceive through the ear and give birth through the mouth. Is that true?"

The weasel stared at Socrates, its jet-bead eyes wide, then sprang from his hand and began to stagger about on the stone floor, whooping with laughter. It collapsed on its side and waved its little paws.

"What a load of vole feathers!" it spluttered. "You lot are really weird, you know that?" Socrates watched, smiling, as it rolled and wriggled in its glee. Then, suddenly, it sprang to its feet and fluffed out its tail. "That's it! Children! Plants make seeds, and animals make babies!"

It took a celebratory munch of crust, its cheeks bulging in a self-satisfied way.

Socrates nodded. "Very true! But some females are unable to bear children, are they not? Are they less alive? And what about those men who choose to share their life with another man, rather than producing fruit in a marriage?"

"Aww, Big Beard. You've got me every which way I turn." It seemed to Socrates that the weasel pouted. "Anyway, I can't hang around here any longer. My life is hunting so I can eat, then eating so I can hunt again." The last of the crust disappeared into its mouth, and its white throat rippled as it swallowed.

"Wait," Socrates said. "Do you have children yourself?"

"Three little ones in the nest," it answered proudly. "How about you?"

"Three children also—boys—but they are grown and able to fend for themselves. My other children, however, are not so strong yet."

"What other children?" the weasel asked over its shoulder, pausing on its journey back to the crack in the wall.

"The children of my mind; my thoughts. I have to die so that they may continue to exist."

"I don't understand," said the weasel, one paw held off the floor. "Your thoughts have no substance. When you die, they won't exist any longer."

"Tell me, weasel, if there wasn't enough food for you and your offspring, what would you do?"

"If they were still suckling…I'd let them die, and then I would eat them," it said in a small voice. "They couldn't survive without my milk, but I could always have more babies." It shifted restlessly, obviously anxious to return to the kittens in its nest, but it did not leave.

"And if they were bigger?"

"If they were on the point of learning to hunt for themselves, then I'd give them every last scrap, honest I would, even if I starved. I'd die happy if I knew I'd set those little guys up for their journey."

Socrates nodded. "Then you understand how it is for me and my reasoning. If I go to my death still believing in those ideas with a full heart, my children go out into the world. Maybe they will survive, and maybe not. But if I renounce my beliefs to save my own skin, it will be as if I turned upon my helpless babies and devoured them."

The weasel crept up to Socrates again and curled at his feet. "And you're ready to die for these thoughts of yours?"

Socrates looked into the liquid eyes above the quivering muzzle, weighed up the value of the noble lie, decided against it, and nodded no. "Willing, perhaps, but not yet ready. I want to see my boys grow up and marry. I want to hold my grandchildren. I'd like to eat a ripe fig just once more before I go to whatever awaits beyond, Hades or black eternal nothing. But that choice has not been given to me."

"It's a paradox," grumbled the weasel. "If you live, you die, but if you die, you live."

"We have reached the end of our journey together, weasel, and discovered what all living things have in common: life seeks to prolong life. By eating in order to survive; by producing children; or by passing on some other reminder of itself, be it creating sculptures, writing plays, or endeavouring to be remembered as just and kind. The mother is prepared to die for her children, the soldier for his country, and I for my philosophy. By passing ourselves on in this way, we make ourselves immortal."

As he spoke, the weasel had fidgeted more and more, wringing its front paws and chittering. Now it burst out:

"Vole feathers! You're crazy! Give up your life—sacrifice your days so that other creatures, not even your own babies, might—*might*, mind you—remember your thoughts and tell them in turn to others? I wouldn't do it. Don't even have time for thoughts, most days. Not a scrap of energy to spare. In fact, I've wasted enough talking to you already." It turned its face from the philosopher and snicked up a couple of crumbs.

"Don't ever stop wondering, weasel," Socrates said to its back. "Now you know the way, you must keep asking questions, and teach your sons and daughters to do the same. People—and weasels—who have ceased to marvel at the world may have hearts that beat and feet that run, but are they truly alive?"

A key turned in the lock. As the heavy door creaked open, the weasel flickered across the floor like a tongue of flame and vanished into the world beyond the wall.

The guard picked up the empty bowl from the floor. "Hope you enjoyed that, O so-called philosopher," he said. "It was your last meal. Hemlock for breakfast. Sleep well, you heretic bastard."

He slammed the door, leaving Socrates alone. The philosopher drew his cloak around him as the cell grew darker. He watched the stars glide past the tiny window, marking his last hours.

The sky was just beginning to lighten when he heard a scuffle and a thump, and made out a russet tail and hindquarters wriggling through the wall.

"Got one!" the weasel announced, shuffling in backwards with all its fur awry. It was tugging a roundish object almost as big as itself, which it tucked under its chin and rolled across the floor to Socrates.

The prize was dusty and bruised from its journey, but when

Socrates split it with his fingers the centre was pink and smelled sweet. He offered a chunk to the weasel.

"No, no, it's yours," it said. "I've got the rest of my life for eating. And for questions! Oh—you insist? Really? In that case..."

Together, in silence, philosopher and weasel explored the nature and meaning of a ripe fig.

7
COLD SCENT

My name is Dutch, and I used to be the best damn nose on the force.

Note: not 'used to have the best nose'. I was the Nose, and the Nose was me.

"Dutch can smell a lie at ten paces," they used to say, and while that wasn't strictly true, I could catch the sour, acid undertones of fear on a suspect's breath, a scent that rose to a crisp point as the untruth in a bunch of half-truths rolled from their mouth. I once had to pick a thief out of a rugby team, right after the match: twelve sweat-soaked men who'd been rolled in mud and pressed together in a grappling mass for eighty minutes, and I was after a single note of scent in that symphony, one fingerprint's worth of smell smeared on the corner of a locker in a changing-room bannered with damp towels and dirty socks. I got him the moment I opened the door.

But that's all over now. Pretty soon, I won't even be 'Dutch' any more. That's just the nickname I got because I'm the only Dutch Shepherd in my unit. Not very imaginative, I grant you, but I liked Dutch a lot better than my real name. Goodbye, Dutch. I'm going to miss you.

On the morning of June sixth, I was proceeding northeast along the A31...

No.

Don't do this like a crime report.

I won't be writing any more of those. I just came in to clear my desk, but when I turned my computer on to wipe the hard drive I found I felt like typing up some sort of record.

Four months, three weeks and two days ago, I was chasing a suspect in my patrol car. It had rained before dawn and the smells were pushing up from the ground like fresh green shoots: young rabbits with the wind in their fur, oak leaves unfurling in the sun. The heavy, viscous smell of spilled diesel, a second too late.

I skidded on the exit of the Shepherd and Flock roundabout, crashed through the barrier and spun across the opposite carriageway. Shrill brakes and the smell of hot rubber before my own fear-sweat drowned everything else.

I woke up two days later with a bandaged head and no sense of smell.

The head healed. The Nose didn't. Post traumatic anosmia, the doctors called it. Severed olfactory nerves don't grow back. The smells are still out there; I can see them rising from a plate of steak or shimmering in diamonds above the dewy grass. But they pass through my nose without sparking a single synapse in my brain, where they used to flash and chime like a fruit machine with spinning reels and bells of smells that tumbled and whirred and lined up and paid out. The scents slide like ghosts through the fine hairs of my nasal passages, wisping off my tongue as I pant them away. I feel like a ghost myself—I can't smell myself, so how do I know I'm even there?

I had a human girlfriend years ago. It didn't work out—these things never do—but we were close for a while, and one night she tried to explain all the colours I can't see. She held up her clothes, wouldn't believe that I couldn't make out which top was orange, which yellow. She spoke of sunsets, gold and pink like a bird's breast; the rustling fire of an autumn forest; the blues and greens and greys that licked foam tips across the wobbling bowl of the sea. Then she felt sorry for me, and there were cuddles. Lots of cuddles.

I tried to tell her about the sense she was missing. I could learn the whole story of her day by holding her top to my nose, never mind what colour it was. And if I rubbed my muzzle and jowls on it, I could carry her image with me, better and more solid than a photo.

She just shrieked "Get off, you slobbery thing!" and tugged the soft cloth from my jaws while I pretend-growled.

Because humans don't get our sense of smell, any more than they know what it's like to have a tail constantly broadcasting your emotions, they fear it and mythologise it. Human crooks go through all sorts of things to cover their scent from the police—ammonia, bleach, mutilate themselves for life some-times—but I can smell through it all.

I *could*.

My human girl used to cover her scent with perfume, civet musk and artificial orange, but I could penetrate her disguise and smell the breadcrumb scent of her skin. It was strongest at the back of her neck, where the hair began, and I liked to lay my muzzle in the base of her skull and just breathe her.

Scent memories. The house where you grew up; the candyfloss and flaking lead paint of a funfair; the chlorinated fear of a school swimming-pool on a bright cold summer day before lunch. The catalogue of smells that make up the girls in my life: the breadcrumb girl, the green-tea girl, the pine cone girl (she was a cat, and a big mistake). All gone.

The Home Office humans tried to insist I take a desk job, but as soon as I knew the Nose was gone for good I put my foot down for early retirement. What good's a desk sergeant who can't smell how his colleagues are feeling, or catch the fading scent of the mugger as he takes down the details of an assault? They'd have me filing the CS cases, the Cold Scents, down in some odourless vault. But my ears are all right. I'd still hear the whispers: there goes Dutch, used to be the best Nose on the force. I was offered counselling and so on, but none of it was going to bring the smells back, so I turned it all down.

This morning I got up, had a shower and put on a clean uniform. Since Becky left I've become paranoid about my own possible stink. I scrub until my pores gape open, lather-rinse-and-repeating the clags of oil and dander from the root of every hair so my brindle fur fluffs up, soft and rain-permeable. I probably don't even smell like Dutch any more. I've shed him like a winter coat, leaving the inner dog exposed: shivering, ridiculous and skinny.

Breakfast was tea and a bowl of cereal. I could taste the sugar in both, but none of the flavour. You don't realise until it's gone that taste is bound up in smell, like a carob bar in a wrapper. Can't open the wrapper, can't get the treat. The cereal crunched and popped in my mouth; I appreciate texture these days, now it's the only way I can distinguish between foods. The tea had a slight oily feel from the tannins.

Becky made me coffee, the morning she went for good. When I reached the dregs she screamed that it was dirt, she'd given me earth and hot water; snatched the mug and threw it at the wall. I've been on tea ever since. It tastes the same to me, delivers the same caffeine hit, and I can be pretty sure a teabag contains nothing but tea. No milk—milk can go sour while it still looks pure and innocent.

She said she was leaving because she couldn't stand my moping, but the truth is I couldn't satisfy her any more. I couldn't smell when she wanted me, what she wanted me to do, or whether she liked it when I did it. She had to guide me all the way, and Becky didn't want to work, just lie back and be worked on.

My walk to the station didn't stimulate me the way it used to. I wasn't looking forward to work, and I couldn't read the passing lines of scent, the sonnets, the limericks, the ballads and the half-rhymes. On the way I passed a young woman with her child in a pushchair and their doggy, a terrier, on a lead. The doggy sniffed my feet, lucky animal, looking up at me with glazed, happy eyes and that permanent smile they all have.

Once I would have known straight away what street they lived on, what they'd had for breakfast, which brand of soap the child's mother had used when she bathed it. Now I couldn't even tell its sex until it blurted "Doggy!" and reached for me, and its mother corrected it.

"No, Paul, that's a dog. A police dog. Buster is a doggy." At the sound of his name, the terrier whirled his stub tail and grinned wider.

I was still in uniform, for today, and community outreach was still one of my duties, so I removed my cap, bent down and allowed Paul to stroke my head, his fingers sticky with some unknown substance I could have identified without trouble five months previously.

"Police dogs are clever, Paul. Remember we read that story about a little girl who got lost, and the nice dog followed her scent and found her? That's what this dog does. He uses his nose."

My teeth smiled, and I put my cap back on.

With no scent cues I almost missed the group of nurses on the other side of the road, three labs and a Newfie, all girls. My ears and tail automatically cocked, and the bitches folded themselves into a giggling, protective pack.

Becky was a nurse, a Labradoodle. Smelled like muffins and daffodils. I feel sorry for her human patients, if she could treat another dog the way she treated me. Maybe she likes humans better.

When I reached the station, Charlie Whiskers was on duty. Cats mostly go in for surveillance stuff, and squeezing into places where they shouldn't be. Not nosework—not *real* policing. We despise them because they don't put their necks on the line, they despise us because we do. But everyone likes fat old ginger Charlie.

"Hello, Dutch! Good to have you back," he said, his white throat throbbing with purr.

"Well, it's not for long. Coming to my leaving do?"

"Wouldn't miss it, my old Dutch. I tried to visit you while you were off, you know, but your girlfriend..."

"Yeah. She's gone now," I told him. He nodded as though he already knew—probably did, Charlie gets all the goss. Didn't say he was sorry. I caught a glimpse of claw as he reached to press the button that would let me through the glass door for the final time.

Have you ever seen a flock of starlings take flight at dusk, among the trees and telephone lines? Thousands of them mass together and swoop apart, rising like fountains, scattering like mercury. The patterns look crazy, but if you're quick and keen you can fix your eye on one individual bird and follow its flight as it shuttles in and out of the web, watching until it stills and roosts. That was the smell of the police station for me, before. Now the air was empty.

I tried to sneak past Jazz's office, but the white shep's nose was in full working order and she boomed my name so I had to go in.

"Morning, Jazz. How's the Peabody enquiry going?" I made sure my face was square to hers and enunciated each syllable.

When Jazz was deafened by a gunshot at close range, she took her move to desk duties gracefully. She used to be my partner, now she's my boss, but I never envied her. Now I'm not so sure. Deafness is easier to mask than a lost sense of smell and she's a good lipreader, though sometimes she talks a little too loudly or mumbles her words.

I used to like her scent, a blend of almonds and marble. In a purely professional, friendly way, of course.

"Rotten. The labs are still working on the evidence, but there's precious little to go on, and the scents are cold now. We'll have to kill the case if we don't get a lead soon."

The shop talk flowed over me like a familiar, snuggly blanket, but I wasn't a part of it any more. I was sealed in my odour-free glass box, untouched and untouchable.

"Don't leave, Dutch!" Jazz yelled suddenly. I flicked my ears, our warning signal, and she overcompensated, dropping to a whisper so I had to bend my head close to hers. "I wish you'd reconsider your resignation. Don't run away from us—we're your friends. We respect you, Dutch! We love you!" She was too loud again, and my ears flattened with embarrassment. She'd said all this before, at various volumes, all the times she'd visited me in hospital and at home. I still wasn't budging.

"You all pity me," I told her, exaggerating the movement of my muzzle so my lips stood away from my teeth and spat her *pity* back in her face. "I don't need your pity."

"Quite right. You need a girl," Dandy said, entering unnoticed among all the shouting. He shook out his long ears with their curls of auburn fur, and smirked.

Dandy is an explosives expert. He lives each day as though it were his last, which it could easily be. 'Bomb dog' is a romantic title, and there's no shortage of volunteers to assist him in his final wishes. It helps that he's a stunning looker, a liver-and-white springer with soulful, liquid eyes that belie his obsessive interest in shagging. He's had an awful lot of final wishes, that one.

"I can't get a girl. No dog would have me, and I'm done with humans. And cats," I added, knowing Dandy would if I didn't.

"You could get a doggy," he suggested, combing his feathered wrist with the claws on his other paw.

I've been on the force fifteen years; I know every filthy joke about dogs and doggies, and *don't* think I haven't noticed which of my colleagues laugh a little too loud and start to sweat between their toes when the subject comes up.

"No thanks," I said, and left the office.

"Tailwagger's Dandy Boy! Try thinking with your *other* brain for a change!" Jazz bawled through the closed door. "The Home Office will chop your balls off if you don't look out!"

Oh, Dandy. Don't ever change.

My unit is mostly sheps and labs, with a few goldens. I used the back doors, which shut out scent until you're there on the floor. The yap of first-cuppa conversation fell silent in an outward ripple from me and my smell. Did I imagine it, or did even the phones stop ringing?

"Morning, boss! Coffee?" Creepy the bloodhound said, whipping the air with his tail. Creepy's another kind of specialist, a cadaver dog. He can nose out a body when it's nothing but a few rags of rotten flesh peeling from a skeleton, even under snow or in running water. Nobody really likes hanging out with him, though. He thinks it's because he smells of death, but the truth is that he's...well, creepy. Bless him, though, for reaching out to the untouchable one, while everyone else acts as if post traumatic anosmia was catching. Part of me has died, I suppose —he's going to be more comfortable with that than the others.

"Tea. Black," I said, and everything went normal, as if I'd given the password.

There'll be a cake somewhere, and a card, disguised in an internal mail envelope as it makes its slow round from in-tray to in-tray. If I could smell I'd already know what flavour icing they'd chosen, but I'd still act surprised and delighted when the box appeared.

I had a mug of tea with the team, letting the talk of scents and trails wash over me. This morning is all business, looking at the open cases and planning action points. Later, when the drink comes out, will be the time for: *"Remember when old Dutch caught the bank robber by tracing the mud on his shoelace"*, and *"That time Dutch smelled the murder weapon in the bonfire and dived in to snatch it out"*. Someone will probably hang up the wretched mirrorball that's been a staple of every office party since long before my time—since dogs started doing police work, probably.

When I could, I excused myself and shut myself into my office with the blind drawn, to clear my desk. Files for the shredder, files for the archive. The work laptop and mobile, the ID card in its wallet, the cap. Empty the pouches of my nylon belt: the Taser, the Speedcuffs, the pepper spray. Good thing I've lost the scent memories or I'd be drowning in nostalgia. As it is, I just feel lighter. Now one last job, while I'm still cleared to check out a firearm.

'Putting him out of his misery', the humans call it, when their doggy or kitty gets old and blind and starts to piddle everywhere. That old blind doggy's probably happier than me—he can still sniff a thousand stories out of a lamp post—but I've got something he hasn't: fingers. And I know how to use them. It'll be rough on Jazz and my team, but with any luck, Creepy'll be the one to find me. He's good at this sort of thing, and…

Charlie Whiskers came in while I was typing that last bit. Sidled through the door without knocking and parked his bum on my desk, swishing his stripy tail. I quickly tabbed into my mail and stared at four months' worth of unread messages.

His little pink nose wrinkled and I worried again that I stank, though what would a cat know?

"You smell nice," he told me. "You're like a cat for cleanliness, these days. What shampoo do you use?"

"What do you want, Charlie?"

He opened the folder in his lap and brought out an old

photo, eight by ten, curly at the edges. Developed from film, not digitally printed. I took it between thumb and finger pads, knowing it smelled of a dozen metals and chemicals, getting none of them. A police unit looked out, eighteen uniformed officers in three rows, their faces bleaching with age.

"But they're humans," I said. "And...doggies." A line of sheps, black or golden, short- and long-coated, sat in front of the humans and grinned with their tongues out.

"Those were just dogs, then. Dogs like you weren't around yet. How did you think they dealt with criminals, before they had us to help?"

"*Humans* were the police? *Humans* put their necks on the line?" I felt outraged, cheapened by the knowledge.

"The other emergency services, too. How did you think society functioned before cats and dogs? Did you think there weren't any crimes? Fires? Accidents?"

"I thought...I didn't think."

Charlie passed me a slim book with a blue cardboard cover. POLICE TRAINING MANUAL, it said in chunky capitals.

I didn't open it. "How did they smell?" I asked, still sceptical.

"Terrible!" Charlie purred with laughter, rocking back and forth on my desk. Then he stopped. Looked me in the eye with his strange slit pupils, fat as an autumn moon now.

"Policing wasn't always about smells, Dutch. Sure, they used the doggies to trace missing persons and criminals on the run. They had their bomb spaniels and bloodhounds. But cases were solved by observation, deduction and legwork. They weren't just walking noses. They were coppers."

"How do you examine evidence properly without smelling it? How could I tell if someone was lying?" I was interested, in spite of myself.

"How can humans tell if someone's lying? By observing their behaviour and cross-checking what they've said with other people. You dogs and your *I am the Nose* stuff!" He shook his head. "You've got a good brain, Dutch. I know you talked to Jazz about the Peabody enquiry. She thinks that because there are no smells left the case is cold, but she's wrong. Prove it! Show your team how things used to be done and can be again. Put your brain in charge of their noses. They need you."

I knew why he was showing me this and I tried not to get hooked. It was cruel of him to give me hope, and a low, catlike trick to appeal to my sense of duty. I sat on my tail to stop it quivering.

"Thanks for the history lesson," I said. But I held on to the book and the photo.

"Promise me you'll look through that manual, at least," Charlie said. He touched my shoulder lightly, dropped to the floor and swayed out.

I stared at the blue cover for a long time before turning over the first page. Whose book was this? How many police humans carried it around with them? What scents was it keeping from me?

Then I began to read.

I didn't look up until I'd finished. After closing the book, I slipped the cuffs and Taser back into my belt.

"Dutch, can I see you for a minute, please?" Jazz has just barked, trying to sound severe, and I heard a giggle from Creepy. They're all out there, with the card and the cake. I don't need to smell it—I deduce it. Time to march in and act surprised, to relish the crisp snow crunch of the icing and the way it melts on my tongue. Then I'll announce that it's not a retirement party after all, and that my arse won't be behind a desk all day either. They'll like that.

My name is Dutch, and I'm going to be the best damn copper on the force.

8

MIDWAY

Counting kept the fox in its place. Takeo had learned the trick as a small boy, when he first had to go to school with a fox cub's skinny tail wriggling indignantly in his shorts leg. Later, he discovered that aviation manuals and technical specifications quieted the animal inside him, too.

So as he hurried across the carrier deck, Takeo counted off the aircraft already in the sky and heading towards the enemy fleet. Ten B5N torpedo bombers and six Type 0 fighters, plus his own and Nobu's still on the deck. That made sixteen; two eights. A lucky number.

An hour before, he had counted off eighteen of the Type 99 dive bombers and six Type 0s; three eights. Lucky again, although not for the ones who hadn't returned.

He ran his gloved hand along the rim of the cockpit, caressing it, as he climbed in. The Zero-fighter was a sleek, cold tube. Men had designed and built every part of it. It had no spirit, until it swallowed its pilot.

The canopy slid shut, muffling the noises of a big, busy ship in motion. He heard the crack of the starter cartridge, and the propeller blurred. Straight away the plane tried to pull itself forward along the deck, but he held back, waiting for the signal to take off.

Once he was cleared, there could be no hesitation. Throttle open, he pointed the howling plane at the spot where the grey deck stopped dead. Before he reached the void, his Zero wobbled into the air and began to climb steadily. The fox within him gave an anxious wriggle.

"My plane has a skin of aluminium alloy," he told it. "It is powered by the Prosperity engine of the Nakajima Aircraft Company."

The fox settled.

Takeo had not dreamed that he would love to fly. Joining the Air Service of the Imperial Navy had felt like a matter in which he had no choice, but he soon understood that the choice had been right for him. The higher he climbed, the lighter his heart. Concentrating on the controls lulled his fox, and he took pride in being one of his squadron's best pilots. After a lifetime spent longing to be ordinary, the desire to excel had surprised him.

The sky, with its few high clouds, had a liquid clarity that made him feel closer to the unseen stars and gods. He thanked them both when he saw that Nobu had also completed his takeoff successfully, and was rising to join him.

Takeo got on fine with the rest of the squadron. They teased him, not only about his need to count everything, but for the way Hana, their mascot, barked and growled when he came near; his pointed face, said to be the shape girls found most attractive; his bottomless appetite for fried tofu. Takeo recognised it as their way of showing friendship, and it pleased him. They might call him a prude because he always insisted on bathing alone, in private, but a prude was better than a coward. Either was better than a demon.

Nobu, though, quietly religious in an old-fashioned way, and quick to blush…Nobu was special. His home village was close to where Takeo had grown up, and Nobu's discovery of the fact early in their training had bonded them. Wherever Takeo flew, Nobu took up the wingman's position, just astern and to the side. The urge to look after Nobu was a pull in Takeo's stomach sharper and more painful than the pull of gravity in a steep dive.

They formed up alongside the rest of the fighter escort, above the slower B5Ns with their torpedoes slung beneath them. Takeo had eaten before takeoff, but he was already ravenous again. The carrier shrank in the distance, a toy boat on a painted ocean brushed in long strokes of blue and white. He unwrapped one of the rice cakes Mother sent him as often as she could—something else the other boys teased him for—and munched it as he steered one-handed. Nobu bobbed up on his right wing, pointing and laughing at his greedy friend. Takeo waved and turned the Zero's nose towards the horizon, at the unseen enemy.

The flavour and texture of bean paste in his mouth recalled Mother so strongly he could almost hear her voice, the day he left for training.

"You could live to be a thousand years old. You could learn to make the foxfire; you could talk to gods and stars. You could fly with no need for a plane, if that's what you want. But you're going to war," she said.

"With everyone else in my class. I want to be like the others." She knew he had to go; she, too, would have felt the tug that summoned him. But mothers had to protest, and she wanted to be an ordinary mother as much as he wanted to be an ordinary son.

"You're not like the others, Takeo-baby. You realise that once you leave home, you can't just be the fox whenever you want?"

"I can't do that now."

"You've always had a safe place here. Out there in the world, you'll be concealing yourself from everyone. You'll sleep alone;

bathe alone. There's no going back, once you make the choice. Man or fox."

She had made that choice when she fell in love with Father. Takeo tried to picture her as a playful cub herself, but she had worn the disguise for so long that it was impossible. She wouldn't even let Takeo see her tail, now, though he had played with it long ago, shifting from cub to toddler as he rolled and bit.

This was the first time she had ever seemed unhappy with her decision.

He didn't tell her that he had said goodbye to the fox earlier that day, as he scampered through fields with the wet grass brushing his belly, rolled in the dappled sunlight of the woods, and ate a fresh offering of hot fried tofu laid on the mossy stones of the ancient shrine. Then he locked away the swiftness, the keen senses, the lithe little four-footed, furry body.

"I've made up my mind," he said, fiercely. "Like you did."

She leaned close. "Are you sure you wouldn't be more comfortable as a girl?" she whispered. "You could still switch. If you do it now."

"Mother!" He turned his head away to hide his pink cheeks. "A girl can't be a pilot!"

"Exactly," she said.

She knelt to hold him tightly, her arms squeezing his shoulders and waist. No—that was the harness, holding him back in his seat as the plane turned, and Takeo was at war.

He counted the aircraft as they began their diving run. The eight—nine—ten torpedo bombers went in low and flat, vulnerable to the anti-aircraft guns of the fleet. Nothing Takeo could do about the flak. The fighters' job was to defend the slower bombers from the enemy in the air.

Flat, matt and angular, the American aircraft carrier was difficult to differentiate from the one Takeo had left behind. He could almost believe they had been tricked by a mischievous spirit into flying in a circle. But there were the foreign fighter planes, looking like koi carp with their plump bodies and short wings. They were moving, trundling along the deck, but so slowly. Takeo could have dived down to pick them off—but that would expose him to the ship's guns, and it was not his job. He counted them off as they lifted, forming groups of four. Nosing past the carrier was the white wake of a torpedo gone wide.

The fifth bomber had now released its load, and was climbing as quickly as it could. The sixth was holding its angle bravely, but the ship's guns tore it to pieces before Takeo's eyes. One wing, then the other, fell blazing to the sea, and the fuselage hurtled low across the deck to cartwheel into the water and sink.

The enemy fighters had gained height, now, and were pursuing the bombers as they climbed away from the fleet. Takeo signalled to the rest of his unit, and they dropped like falcons on pigeons.

Everyone knew the Grumman was no match for Japan's Type 0. A tight turn delivered the first one into Takeo's sights, and he shot it down methodically, with the minimum of ordnance. Three squeezes of the trigger; three five-second bursts. The next plane flashed its vulnerable underside to him as it turned to flee. He placed bullets along its belly, and shot away part of the tail. That was two.

He turned and twisted, never staying in one line of flight long enough to be a target. His view grew confused, with the horizon rolling and planes crossing his vision faster than he could count them. He looked for his wingman, but could not locate him.

Always, when he was anxious, the fox rose in him. He felt it surge through his veins, trying to sharpen his teeth and nails for a fight it couldn't understand. Fox breath whined between his teeth.

There was Nobu—the way he crouched over the controls, intent, was unmistakable. The fox hunkered down, only to surge up again as Takeo saw the Grumman lumbering up behind his wingman, who was too focused on his own target to notice.

"Nobu! Look out!"

Takeo was already diving to chase the American away. He saw Nobu jump at the anguished voice over his radio, and glance over his shoulder. Now he was flicking his plane from side to side, but the American was too close to be shaken off. One of the Zero's cockpit panes starred and went white, like ice, and Takeo closed on the Grumman. The other pilot chose to escape by a steep descent. Takeo let him go. Kills were important—he mouthed a silent tally of his score so far—but Nobu more so. He moved up to his slot ahead and beside the other pilot.

As he dropped into position, the Zero shuddered under a succession of hits. Takeo had left his own tail vulnerable. The rudder went wrong, so he had to stamp down hard to stay level. The smell of fuel was sudden, and startling to heightened senses.

"Wingspan twelve metres!" he yelled, tearing his oxygen mask away from his face so the radio would not broadcast his panic. "Length nine metres!" He prickled under his flightsuit as fur licked along his arms. The tail, outraged at its confinement, plumped up and thrashed. Clapping the mask back over his nose and mouth, Takeo breathed deeply. His heart pattered, like a small, trapped animal's.

"Empty weight...empty weight, um..." He imagined the fox loose in the cockpit, struggling in the heavy folds of the flightsuit. Tiny paws scrabbling at the release lever as the flames rose. Charred fox bones in a cage of twisted metal at the bottom of an ocean, for a thousand years. As far as one could be from the stars and the gods.

"Takeo? Takeo!"

A shrill whine was all the answer and reassurance he had for his wingman. Nobu! Nobu must be saved! But Takeo, who had not lived long enough to grow wise, could not even save himself.

Smoke streaming along the wings. Fuel slopping over his feet. The fox keening, struggling to break free. *Count.* Counting always helped. Ten, fourteen, twenty bullet holes in the cockpit. Four, three, two—the reading on the altimeter falling as the minutes of flight left to him ticked lower with every spurt of fuel.

He had no strength left to hold the fox back. Well, then, let it enjoy the heights, briefly. Reaching up with his left hand, he loosened his oxygen mask.

The muzzle poked free, black nose questing at the thin air. The prickling of his forearms became unbearable, and he pulled off the gauntlets to reveal smooth fur. In Takeo's vision, the sunlight grew brighter, the shadows deeper. Where there was movement his eyes snapped to it, and he could follow the planes that filled the sky as if he were idly watching so many flies crawling on a wall.

Rubbery pads took the stick in a sure grip, and a claw rested on the fire button. The heavy boots slid off his feet, and paws kicked the rudder pedals. Fox reflexes spun the Zero. An enemy fighter plunged into the sea.

Takeo's tail thrashed again, but this time he recognised the motion as communicating excitement, not terror. The fox he had kept shuttered down all this time—the fox *wanted* to fly! Of course it did—it was part of Takeo, after all! His mind, his body, overlaid with fox.

He aimed and fired ahead of one of the Grummans, watching the arc of bullets curl backwards and strike perfectly along the fuselage. The American planes could take a lot of punishment, more than the Zero, but they had limits. Flame lit the sea-grey body, and the aircraft plunged. Takeo slung his own plane sideways and down through the gap it left.

"Nobu follow me!" he barked into the mask slung from his neck. His voice was hoarse and thick. Nobu lined up on his tail, obedient, unquestioning, like the good wingman he was.

Takeo's eyes flicked and darted as he sought a path through the dogfight. He tipped the wing, rolled the Zero on its axis, soared past, above, between the turmoil. Nobu's plane seemed stuck to his own, just the way they had trained together. He turned away from the sun, to where the Japanese fleet must lie.

The battle faded behind them, so that the two aircraft, and their shadows on the water, were the only moving objects from horizon to horizon. The clouds sulked, motionless, and at this height the sea seemed frozen. In the cockpit, the needle of the fuel gauge moved steadily down. The beat of the engine was sound. There was no threat in sight.

Takeo remained half-fox.

Ravenous again, he ate the last of his snacks; studied his compass, hoped that it was reading true. The sea crawled by. Takeo gazed down at their two shadows joined tail to nose as they bumped across the waves.

For a long time there was no change, then the shape elongated and separated. The rear portion grew larger. The other Zero was dropping behind, losing height as it lagged.

"How are you doing, Nobu?"

The answering crackle was faint. "My eyes…blood, I think…"

"Can you still see me?"

"Just."

"Then follow. And keep your nose up."

Ten more minutes, and still only open water below them. Surely they should have reached the carrier by now? He scanned the horizon with a predator's eyes, and made out the floating speck that meant safety.

Safety for Nobu, at least. Takeo could not walk among the other pilots like this, and he had no idea how he might transform back. He could circle for a while to buy time, pretending there was a fault with the landing gear, but he had too little fuel to do so for long. Perhaps if he ditched, he could paddle the life raft to some secluded island and live on crabs and fish until he changed back, or forever. Perhaps he would sink to the bottom of the sea still strapped in with his secret.

"Takeo?" The voice in his ears was faint.

"You land first," he told Nobu. "My plane's in better shape than yours."

"I can't see! It's all dark!"

On the deck of the carrier, they were making ready for the two planes, creating space among the battered survivors already landed. Takeo lined his nose up and dropped his landing gear.

He would not lose Nobu to the sea now, nor to a crash on the deck. He would *not*. He bristled, his fur standing on end. Electricity crackled in each hair, and the needles on the cockpit dials swung back and forth. His trapped tail writhed against his leg. Claws gripped the stick.

Yet the picture that came to him—in the middle of the spinning, the sickly fuel smell, the noise and smoke—was of the little mossy shrine, and the fresh offering upon it.

Foxfire filled the cockpit with a bright, white glow.

"Can you see me now, Nobu?"

"Yes! Yes, I can!"

"Good." Takeo shook himself from nose to tail, and his forepaws on the stick guided the Zero down to the deck of the carrier.

The two young men lay side by side in the bath, their bodies blurred beneath the foam. Beyond the door were all the sounds and smells of a busy hospital, but the scent of soap and the splash of water blocked them out for now.

The deep cuts above Nobu's eyes were healing and he had been passed fit to fly, but he was unhappy. Takeo saw it in the set of his mouth. He knew the disgrace of the lost battle, a defeat which had been reported in no news broadcasts or papers, was weighing on his wingman.

Takeo had not even been allowed to contact his mother. She'd know he was safe, because she would have sensed his death. That was some comfort, but no contact meant meant no food parcels, and he was faring badly on the hospital rations. He felt a pang that might equally have been hunger, an uneasy fox, or homesickness.

Entirely human ears would have missed the quiet sigh beside his ear, but Takeo turned his head. "What's the matter, Nobu?" he asked.

"I had an interview today. They're reassigning the survivors to new units. What if they split us up?"

That was Nobu's worry? Takeo felt his body flush with proud, embarrassed heat, like the needle stab of fur.

"They won't split up two pilots who work well together," he told Nobu. Somehow, they would not. The fox would find a way. "There'll be other battles, and we'll be in them. Together." He did not promise they would win.

When Nobu still frowned, Takeo splashed water in his face to make him blink and laugh, but the other boy would not be distracted.

"Takeo? When I followed you back to the carrier, you were sort of glowing."

"You were half blinded," Takeo said. His tail stirred beneath him and he plunged his hand below the surface to still it.

"And after we landed, some of the crew said you looked strange," Nobu continued.

Takeo's spine pricked. But by the time they forced the cockpit open and pulled him out, there had been nothing out of the ordinary to see. Anything glimpsed as he landed part-transformed would have been a brief, strange sight indeed, and impossible to corroborate. He was safe.

"One of the doctors here was asking me questions, while you were asleep." Nobu poked him in the ribs. "He said you fought when he tried to undress you. Are you really so shy, Takeo?"

That was a bold question from someone who was shy himself. Takeo let the water lap at his chest. His limbs began to tingle, and his lips moved as he recited lengths and widths like a prayer, and counted blossoms on the tree outside the window. Yet, here he was, sitting naked next to his friend. He would not have allowed this if the fox did not feel safe. He relaxed against the tiled edge of the bath, as if he was settling into the cockpit.

"Nobu, listen. Before you joined the military, you prayed at your family shrine for divine help to protect you."

Nobu's face was already rosy from the hot water, but now he flushed a deeper pink. "How do you know?"

"Because I am the help you prayed for." He took his friend's hand and guided it below the surface, closing it around the damp cylinder of his tail. "My family has been tied to yours for a long time."

Nobu's eyes widened, but he didn't speak, and he didn't let go of the tail.

Relaxed by the water, and Nobu's trust, Takeo allowed his ears and face to lengthen. Fur bloomed along his arms and legs, to sway like waterweed in the warm current. Nobu's face was a perfect mix of amusement and wonder. Takeo wriggled his tail, enjoying the sensation of another's touch upon it, and grinned with pointed teeth.

He was a fox and he was a fighter pilot, and he was both

together. He had made the foxfire, and now he would practise until he could make it at his own will and control its power, as easily as he fired the Zero's guns. His cockpit radio brought him voices as remote as gods and stars. He might not yet have a thousand years' worth of wisdom, but he could fly without magic. No matter what the rest of this losing war brought them, he would keep Nobu safe.

9

A BLACKER DOG

Contrary to legend, the black dog doesn't come looking for you. It's already there. Most people just don't see it until the right moment, but I'm not most people. I often wish I was.

"What do you reckon, Hunter?"

My partner gets down on all fours to examine the woman's body. Her own black dog is long gone. According to Hunter, his kind is never out of work for long. Someone's always getting born.

"I don't think this is about insurance fraud any more," he says.

"Thanks, Hunter. Thanks a million."

Hunter can't say if assignments are random or tailored. If they're specific to the individual, I don't want to know why I got a portly black Labrador in a trench coat and dark glasses, whose greatest joy in life is pepper jerky. As I watch, he sucks in the end of his current stick, chews, and swallows.

"Sorry, Jon. You know I can't do much without another dog to talk to."

"I'll call the police."

Bodies weren't part of the plan for today, and the water's got too deep and murky for a little fish like Jon Mazza. 'Private detective' is what I put on my tax form, and enter online when I'm asked to fill in my occupation (it never shows up in the dropdown box, for some reason), but the bulk of my work comes through this big property firm. I find out whether fires, missing deliveries, workplace injuries and other assorted incidents and accidents are just people being people, or people being dishonest people. I am, when I'm being an honest person myself, a loss adjuster.

The building I'm in is an old Victorian property, like all the houses on this street that didn't go in the Blitz. It's been split into flats, but the land it stands on, and the neighbouring plot that's been sold already, would be worth more with a new development on it. You can fit a lot more tenants in those purpose-built jobs. All that was standing in the way was the fact that the house was a listed building; try to knock it down and the entire community's up in arms. Unless it catches fire first. Convenient for everyone except the owner.

And, apparently, someone else.

The body isn't burned or even marked. Smoke inhalation, I tell myself. Just like a proper detective. We're way up on the attic floor, and nothing in this room caught fire, but the smell of smoke has drifted in and a fine coating of ash has settled on the floor. Hunter sneezes and shakes his ears. It's an affectation; his paws leave no imprint in the ash, so he can't be breathing it in. He's just messing around because he doesn't know what to do.

When I was a kid, I thought having Hunter would make me the best detective in the world. He could talk with other black dogs and give me the skinny, whatever that is, and I'd solve the case as if by magic. It works sometimes, and I've had a few successes, but it's hard when you can't explain how you got your evidence without bringing mythical beasts into it. Hunter has his moments, sure, but mostly he's a big, useless lump with meat breath. He couldn't even tell me my wife was having an affair.

When the police arrive, the little attic gets crowded. There are two officers, a constable and an inspector, and that means two black dogs too. Only Hunter and I can see them as they cram themselves in. One is an all-black Dobermann, but the inspector's is a minute Pomeranian. Hunter and I have often discussed whether your dog has a paw in what you'll be when you grow up. They tend to be short discussions, because he can't stand it when I use expressions like 'has a paw in'.

"Yo," the Pom says to Hunter. "That your human? Did he do it?"

"No, he didn't. And he can see us, so shut your yap."

She growls, but subsides. Hunter seems to have some kind of seniority over other black dogs. He's not sure, but he thinks he's been around a long time, gone through a fair number of human lives. Maybe that's why he likes to walk on two legs, too, and wear clothes. Or maybe that's just his weird sense of humour.

The constable takes my details along with a brief statement. I'm glad I haven't touched the body; Hunter always takes care of that side of things for me. No prints. The Dobermann leans against his legs and looks up at him adoringly from glowing red eyes. I wince—what if those eyes meet his? That's why Hunter wears shades.

"Something the matter, Mister Mazza?" It comes out like a tongue-twister, but he keeps a straight face. I shake my head.

The black Pom is sniffing around the attic, poking her head and paws into every nook and cranny. Some of them are like that, getting involved with their people's lives. Suddenly she stiffens, yaps so hard her tiny paws lift off the floor, and starts trying to stuff herself into a gap between two boxes. Her paws scrabble helplessly, unable to touch whatever it is she's seen, and her yaps take on a plaintive tone.

"I think there's something down there," I say, to put her out of her misery. I'm rewarded with a suspicious stare, but the constable pulls the boxes apart and tweezers something—a crumpled piece of paper, it looks like—into a plastic bag. I'm familiar enough with police work to know it's probably nothing. Rather than thank me, the little dog turns to Hunter.

"How come…?" she asks.

"Don't know. He was born that way."

They hold eye contact for a few seconds. Hunter's jaws work away at a jerky stick; the Pom's nose twitches. I've no idea what's passing between them, but at the end of it she gives a little *snuf* and trots over to her inspector.

"Mister Mazza?"

"Sorry. What did you say?"

"I said, report to any police station within the next seven days with your documentation. And don't leave the country, please."

I have no intention of going anywhere. I'm involved now.

Although I could report to any police station, I look up the collar number of one of the officers and go to that one. While I give my statement, Hunter prowls off in search of the officers we met at the house—and their dogs. By the time I've finished, he's back at my side, breathing hot jerky breath down my neck. How he does that, when he has no other physical presence… well, it's annoying, but it's usually the least of my worries.

He falls into step beside me as we walk to the bus stop.

"Did you find the Pom?"

"Her name's Delphine."

"Ooh!" I elbow him in where his ribs would be if I could touch him. He's never shown this level of interest in a girl dog before.

"Do you want to know, or not?"

"Please."

"The dead woman was an employee of Hutch Estates."

The developers trying to buy the land. This is almost like a real case. Complete with the fact that I have absolutely no reason to get involved.

"Obviously they're investigating the company, who are obviously denying any involvement."

"Obviously." I grin at Hunter, who glares back—at least, his eyebrows lower over his glasses.

"I know that look," he says. "Why not just do the job you're paid for?"

"What's up, Hunter? I thought we both wanted to be proper detectives. To make a difference. Now this thing's dropped in our laps, aren't you the least bit interested? Don't you want to make absolutely sure there hasn't been a murder right under our noses?"

He doesn't answer. He's sometimes sensitive about body part metaphors, given his incorporeality.

"Anyway, the police won't let me do the job I started, now." The fire has already cost my employers, the company that owns the current flats, a hell of a lot; they've had to put the tenants up in a hotel, and they'll also be liable for destroyed and damaged possessions. Now they're faced with the choice between rebuild and replace, a big job that will leave them out of pocket even after the insurers cough up, or simply selling the land to Hutch. It all seems petty now a life's been lost.

"What was her name?" I ask.

He looks at me, knows I want to look into this properly. I know him, too, and I can tell he doesn't want me to. Hunter used to be as keen on playing detectives as I still am, and I wonder what's wrong. Eventually he gives a doggy sigh with a little squeak in it, raises his eyebrows above the glasses, and tells me; "Phoebe Knight."

I spend my evening tracking Hutch Estates through the news sites. It does something to keep the image of the body away.

I'd always thought their name was a subtle joke, but it turns out there really is a Mr. Hutch at the helm. He smirks out of a photo on the *"About Us"* page of the company website from a private office with paintings on the walls and an ornate dagger on the coffee table. The slightly creepy human side of the business, ready to help you find the home of your dreams—for a price.

A high price for some people, it turns out. Go through the news archives for the last ten years and the name of Hutch Estates pops up a number of times in connection with deaths and accidents. Purely incidentally, of course. More than a decade ago, fewer newspapers were online. If I want to go any further down this alley, I'll have to wait till morning and get my lazy self to an actual library.

Hunter is uncharacteristically quiet while all this is going on. He looks over my shoulder occasionally, and paces the carpet, and munches jerky sticks. Eventually, he says:

"Don't you think you should leave this to the professionals?"

"What's up? Squeamish about dead bodies? You'll be seeing mine sooner or later."

We both know it, but rarely bring it up in conversation. His silence is hacking me off, though.

"Yeah, and I'd rather it was later." He scratches his ears, fiercely. "Could be centuries before I get another human I can talk to. Longer before I get one I'd want to."

He doesn't know enough about himself or the rest of his kind to know how rare my so-called gift might be. He doesn't often reveal it to other dogs, the way he did with the Pom... sorry, with *Delphine*.

"You just want to stick with me so you can see more of Delphine."

"Shut up."

"Have you thought this thing through? I'm sure the officer's very nice, but I might run out of small talk on a double date."

Black dogs can't stray far from their people. We found that out the first time my mum instructed me to leave my imaginary friend at home while I went to school. That's when I learned to lie, and Hunter learned just how much he could torment me if reacting to him would get me in trouble.

"Give it a rest." Hunter flashes yellow teeth.

"Put a jerky stick in it."

"*Fine.*" He snaps one in two and crams both halves into his muzzle. Crumbs fall, but vanish before they hit my carpet.

He wanders off after that, inasmuch as he can. He's out of my eyeline, and quiet, so I can't tell if he's sleeping or thinking or what. It must be dull for him, being tethered to a sedentary bloke like me. Sometimes I turn the TV on for him.

I carry on browsing, waiting to get sleepy. There isn't a peep out of Hunter while I browse, but suddenly I smell jerky, and when I turn round, he's right there; nose almost on my neck.

"Could you...not be creepy, *please?*"

He backs off and takes a chair. Presumably he hovers just above it; I've never been able to figure that out, but he looks convincing enough, straddling the seat with his arms on the backrest. His mouth is a grim line, and I'm suddenly frightened.

"Jon, don't be scared, but I'm going to take the shades off."

"But I feel fine!"

That's a lie. My chest hurts, my stomach's squeezing, my hands feel cold and damp. I'm dying. Heart attack? No—this has all come on since Hunter spoke. It's just harmless old fear; I think I'm going to die, so I'm freaking out. Hunter hasn't moved since his warning. What kind of sick joke is he pulling this time?

Nothing happens. Hunter waits, silent and motionless, while my heart rate slows and my stomach settles down. Even his jaws, usually mumbling away at a jerky stick, are still. Only the fine whiskers on his muzzle flutter with his breath. Nothing is still happening. I let out my breath. I'm alive.

"I can't kill you just by looking at you, Jon," he says at last. "That's not my power. It has to be the right time."

"What? You always let me think..."

"I only started wearing the glasses because my eyes made you cry when you were little. And it came in useful to have you think I could kill you any moment. Still does, sometimes." He at least has the decency to look ashamed at that.

"I remember you sitting next to my cot," I tell him. "I was crying because I couldn't touch you."

"You were a cute baby."

He whips the sunglasses off his nose. I squeeze my eyes shut and bury them in the crook of my elbow, then, embarrassed, peer over the top.

His *eyes*. I've seen other black dogs, of course, with their eyes glowing among the dark fur like lit coals, but I've never let my gaze linger, just in case. Looking at Hunter, now, I see I was wrong. Those aren't coals, they're holes. Tunnels straight to the pit of Hell. My silly, funny, lifelong companion and friend has a direct eyeline to the devil.

They're like lasers, a light so intense the red burns back to black at the centre and leaves a green splotch when I close my eyes. I'm scared that if I stare too long I'll go blind, but warm dog-breath blows across my face, whispering "Open your eyes! *Open* them! *Jon!*"

I unsqueeze my eyelids a fraction, peering out between the lashes like I'm trying to cheat at *Hide and Seek*. Hunter's nose is up against mine, so close I can see the pores glinting with moisture and the little hooks of his whiskers. Is his muzzle going grey? Can he even age?

His paw sweeps upwards, and even though he can't touch me, my chin follows until I'm looking him square in the eyes. I get to my feet, back away slightly. He stands too; eyes locked on mine. We're exactly the same height. I never noticed.

My attempts to distract myself from those eyes aren't working. I try to focus on them, but my brain can't quite figure out where the focal point is. It's like staring down twin tunnels. The red points, pupil-less, seem to shift and waver around. I feel myself going hot and prickly, although the hairs on my arms are standing up on end.

"Jon," Hunter's voice seems to come from a long way off. The heat is flushing my face and making my heart race. "Jon, I can't hurt you, and neither can my eyes. They're weird, and scary, but they're not fatal. All right? Trust me."

And I do, because he's been the one constant in my life. A constant that nobody else can see, but if I stop believing I'll know I'm mad. I stare until Hunter is just Hunter, his tummy bulgy under his trench coat, his tail poking stupidly out of the hole in the back. My best friend. My partner. Sure, he has two glowing holes in his face, but nobody's perfect.

Hunter puts his shades back on. The room seems to grow lighter, and I realise I have a headache. I set about going to bed, pottering around in and out of the bathroom while Hunter, who doesn't have a bedtime ritual (certainly not brushing his teeth) lounges against the wall and watches. When I get into bed, he shrugs off his coat and curls up on it, turning around to get comfortable.

"Why did you do that?" I don't mean the turning around—he's been doing that ever since I can remember—and he doesn't even pretend he thinks I do.

His paw tilts the frame of the glasses forward a fraction, so I get a searing flash of red that makes me blink, then replaces them.

"Because if you're going to go through with this, and if this is what I think it is…you needed to see what I've just shown you, and know what I've just told you."

"Well, thanks, I guess. Good night, Cryptic Dog."

"Good night, Silly Human."

I could get used to this proper detective stuff. Unfortunately, none of it is working. I never see Hutch arrive at the offices of his eponymous company, or leave them, despite long hours on stakeout. I'm no stranger to waiting—a lot of my work catching out benefits cheats involves lurking outside their houses, poised to photograph them in the act of something a person with a bad back couldn't manage—but after a week, it's dispiriting. Besides, nobody is paying me for this. It's amazing how the thought of an hourly rate can liven up sitting in a car for hours. I drop in on the pretext of looking for a luxury docklands penthouse, but I can only really do that once. Hunter tries snooping around while I do, but he can't get far enough in without me following.

I get a little of my paying work done in the evenings, on the internet, but a lot of my time is taken up trying to glean information about Hutch online. He has a business profile with links to a few contacts, but nothing personal. Nobody tags him in photos. He doesn't have a gym membership and he doesn't seem to stay at hotels. Even his home address is a mystery. I can only work on the personal data that companies are legally able to sell, and he's been careful about giving that away. He must really hate getting junk mail.

It's Hunter who gets me my interview with Delphine's inspector. We've gone through what I'm going to say—the big black furry idiot thinks he knows my job better than I do, now —but none of it has any effect until he takes the black Pom aside and whispers to her. Whatever he's saying makes her quiver a bit, then she jumps up into her human's lap and snuggles in. The inspector can't see her own black dog, or feel her, even when Delphine is licking her hand, but something must be getting through because her attitude shifts from unhelpful to, "*I'll think about it*", and then to letting me accompany me her to Hutch's office. After lunch. It's practically a date, now.

Hunter insisted it had to be the inspector, too, when any uniformed officer would have got me through the doors. He's gone all professional again, but he is never going to hear the end of this Delphine business.

Lunch isn't a date. I've blagged my way into it with wild claims of being able to provide evidence against Hutch (I have no idea what this evidence might be, and I really hope Hunter has), and now Inspector Ruxley—her first name is Ann—just wants a chance to decide whether I'm genuine or a nutter. It is not easy to prove the former, when at least half my mind is on Hunter and Delphine. They are definitely flirting, and I don't know whether to be disturbed (Hunter walks on two legs, and wears clothes, and it feels wrong that he's hitting on what is to all appearances a dog, albeit a talking, invisible one) or amused.

"Just as long as you understand the risks," I hear him say.

I have to cover a laugh at this outrageously old and corny trick. Oh baby, I'm so wild and dangerous!

"Jon?" (I begged Ann to drop the 'Mr. Mazza' stuff as soon as we left the police station.)

"Sorry, what?"

"I asked why you were so interested in this case."

"Oh—just a hunch." Now I'm coming out with the corny lines, too. But she nods.

"I think more police work revolves around hunches than any of us want to admit."

By the time lunch finishes, I don't want it to. I've been in a pleasant little bubble that definitely is *not* any sort of double date, and as far as I'm concerned, the real world can get stuffed; but Hunter is already at the door, staring out at the rain. He's not wearing his shades any more; hasn't since the night we practised gazing into each other's eyes. Delphine skips after him and, as if attached to an invisible lead, Ann puts her credit card away and stands.

Every time I've tried to enter the Hutch Estates, I've been

sent away with a flea in my ear and my tail between my legs; or so I told Hunter, to annoy him. Ann just walks in and shows her ID.

"We'd like to see Mr. Hutch, please."

And, just like that, we're in. The receptionist talks urgently on the phone, too low for us to hear although Hunter pricks up his ears, then we're being led through a door I didn't even notice on my reconnoitring trip, along a corridor, and into the office from the About Us picture. All that fine detective work hitting the search engines, and what I should have done is visit the nearest adult shop for a police uniform.

Hutch, like his office, is exactly as he appears in his website photo. Greying hair; lined, aristocratic face; dark eyebrows. What the website didn't show, because it won't show up in photos (I tried often enough with Hunter, as a boy) is the black dog at his side.

It's not any breed I recognise, though if I had to pick I'd probably go for 'hellhound'. And it's *black*, blacker than black. Hunter's coat has that well-fed Labrador gloss to it. This dog's fur is like sharkskin, reflecting no light. I can barely make out the haunches and the massive paws; it looks like one block of shaggy, malevolent darkness. Seated, its head comes up to Hutch's chest. The head itself is as big as his, something like a wolf crossed with a mastiff, with brows eerily similar to Hutch's overhanging the—*don't look at the eyes!*

Hutch sees me looking. And he knows what I'm looking at.

"I always wondered if there were others," he says, and his dog's tongue comes out, blacker than a Chow Chow's. I expect it to be forked like a snake's but it's an ordinary dog tongue, poking over big yellow teeth, and a dribble of drool confirms it. Its tail thumps once; it's long and thin, like a greyhound's, and this is somehow the most disquieting thing of all.

"Others?" Ann asks, making me jump. Ten minutes ago we were sharing lunch and I was indulging in mild romantic fantasies; now I'd forgotten she was there. Hutch, though, beats me in the discourtesy stakes by not even acknowledging the police officer's presence.

Delphine is circling the bigger dog, unsure what to do. Hunter stands at my shoulder, but every hair on his body, at least those not hidden by his trench coat, is standing on end, and his tail is trying to tuck itself between his legs. I've never seen him like this before. I've never imagined a situation where he couldn't take control, wise, implacable and protective.

"We have evidence that you were involved in the deaths..." My voice is a croak. There is no evidence, and I don't know where I thought Hunter was going to pull it from. He lied to bring me here, so he could...what? Turn me over to this man and his terrifying dog?

It can't kill me. I remember that from Hunter's little pep talk. It can't kill me.

It kills Ann.

That great head snakes around and the red eyes target her like lasers, so I can see their glow flicker across her face. She frowns, brushes the hair from her forehead, and turns in the direction of whatever she's sensing. I shout a warning, but her eyes widen and I know she's seen it.

Hutch's dog shocked me, and I've been seeing the black dogs all my life. I can't imagine what it must be like for Ann in the brief time between the apparition and her hands going to her chest as she sinks to her knees and topples face forwards.

Delphine shrieks as though every bone in her is being crushed, and runs to her human. But before she can reach Ann, her body starts dissolving like ash and wisps away in black smoke.

At least she'll come back, unlike her human.

"Now we can talk," Hutch says pleasantly.

It's not him I want to talk to. It's Hunter. Hunter who told me only your own black dog can open the door between life and death, and even that only at the right time. He lied *again*. But one look at him and I see he didn't know he was wrong. He's panting with distress, and the pale rims of his eyes are showing around the red.

"It's nice, isn't it? Having a lifelong companion? A secret nobody knows?" His hand reaches down and he caresses the air above his dog. They can't touch each other, any more than Hunter and I can, but it leans into the stroke and rumbles, ears submissive. "I thought I'd use mine to make money. While you are...a loss adjuster? You've visited my office a couple of time in the last week."

"I'm a private detective."

"How sweet. A boy and his dog."

"You're killing people over the *property* market?"

"It's a very lucrative market. And I don't kill people often. You have to be careful. Mostly I use Kharon here to find information for me, and to influence my business contacts. It's a little like being a private detective, I imagine."

His grin tells me that he knows exactly how good I am at being a detective, and I wish I'd made a better stab at it. My standing is pitiful compared to his, though at least I have the moral high ground by several thousand feet.

"You killed Ann."

"The autopsy will say she had a heart attack."

"And Phoebe Knight. Your own employee."

"Sooner or later, someone was going to get too curious for their own good about my methods."

"You killed her and dumped her body in the flats before you started the fire. How are you planning to get away with that?"

"Ah, smoke inhalation. I was pleased with that one."

Kharon's mouth opens, and black smoke dribbles down to drift along the floor. I can smell it, bitter and dangerous. A glance at Hunter tells me he's never seen anything like this. All he can do is make infinite jerky sticks appear. Now I think of it, this is the longest I've ever seen him go without one. Tricky to eat when your jaw's hanging open.

Hutch hasn't lasted this many years by bumping someone off every other day. It's a classic pattern: killer kills once, then again to cover their tracks, or because the first time was so easy. Eventually they get so desperate or hardened that more killing seems the only way out, and they up the pace. Phoebe Knight, then Ann, all in a matter of days. And now, almost certainly, me.

"There are rules." Hunter speaks for the first time, and I can tell it's an effort. I've never seen his ears so low.

"It speaks! What's your name, then?"

"Why don't you guess? You know everything else about me." I don't want him to know Hunter's name. That just feels too... intimate. Hunter must agree, because his jaw snaps shut.

"As for the rules, we've been breaking them all my life." The dog's ears perk at the 'we'. It looks pleased, and reveals even more teeth. "I started when I was a boy, by changing his name. Then the training began."

"You can't do that." Hunter's voice is flat, but I've known him long enough to recognise the note of panic behind it. It's the voice he used when I scared myself into almost drowning at the beach, and he had to talk me back up onto the sand.

"You need a strong will to disobey, and a stronger one not to pop out of existence once you have."

He leans back and smirks, and the dog Kharon tips its head up in an ecstasy of pride and love.

"I could teach you, if you like. Your dog's a little tubby, but he can train. Would you like that, boy? Like to influence the world around you with more than your mouth? You've got such a wonderful opportunity here, both of you. Stick with me and I'll show you."

Here's where we pretend to go along with his scheme until we can get out of this and get Hutch arrested. Unfortunately, Hunter didn't get the memo. He's so used to nobody being able to hear him except me, he's got lippy. And now it will be the death of both of us.

"That's not what I'm for and it's not what *he's* for," he snarls. "You! Kharon! Snap out of it and do your job, you peabrain!"

I wonder if, despite the dog's size and sinister appearance, it's actually as dim as Hunter is suggesting. It hasn't said a word, just smouldered and menaced. And *I* wouldn't let a slimeball like Hutch mould me into a tame executioner. I hope.

"Kharon, kill them. The human first, so the dog can watch."

I jerk my head away and stare fixedly at the ceiling. A lifetime of dodging red eyes doesn't go away overnight, in spite of Hunter.

"Jon. *Look at him.*"

Hunter has lied, or been mistaken, so much today that I have no reason to trust him. No reason, except the whole of our lives together. And if he's wrong Kharon will kill him as well, and I don't want to live without my invisible partner. I turn my head slowly, peeking out between my eyelashes.

Looking into Kharon's eyes is like getting close to an incandescent lightbulb. After only a few seconds, I can't tell the eyes from the dancing green ghosts they leave on my vision. The rest of the room seems to dim, and there's a sharp smell like the head of a match. My ears are buzzing, and I'm hot all over.

"He can't kill you. It's not time." So far away, Hunter's voice, and so sad. I look at Kharon, crouched and bristling, staring at me with such sizzling heat its eyes are turning white.

*If looks could kill...*I think, and want to giggle.

Outside the walls of this room, the rest of the world is carrying on its business. I can hardly imagine it. This, here, this is the whole world, this is the only thing that matters— and that's when I realise. This is the job Hunter and I have to do, to get rid of this hellish partnership that's upsetting the natural order of things. It's why we were put together and why I can talk to him. We should have spent all our time practising for this moment, not messing around and bickering. Too late now.

The heat washes over me, but it doesn't hurt. It's like putting my hand close to a flame, but not too close. As long as I keep Hunter's reassuring voice in my mind, I'm fine. Everything's fine. I hold Kharon's baleful stare, and smile in the face of the black dog.

I've been thinking so much about dogs, I forgot people can be dangerous too.

"Switch," calls Hutch. Kharon's gaze flicks away. I blink and shiver, out of that heat, that light. I'm only just ready for Hutch and the knife he's grabbed, the one from the website picture. I shift my body left and catch him as he comes. Even as the pain arcs along my side, I realise he knows this is the showdown. He can't explain away a stabbing in his own private office, performed with his own private property.

I've never been stabbed before. I want to recoil from the shock and pain and just curl up in a ball, but my body has too much forward momentum and I grapple Hutch to the floor, twisting his arm back so he's forced to drop the knife. As we roll and wrestle, I try not to notice how much blood there seems to be on our clothes, our hands, the carpet.

A second pain cuts through me, and I think Hutch has another weapon, but he's pulled away, grabbing at his own chest. We turn together to where Hunter and Kharon are standing nose to nose. Their eyes are locked on each other's, and there's a hum coming off them that sets my teeth on edge, like a high voltage cable running through the room.

There's no way Hunter can win this. Whatever it is. He's pudgy and silly where Kharon is a honed killing machine. Does it work both ways—will I pop out of existence when he goes? Then Hutch will be free to do as he likes. Nobody else will have any idea how to stop him. I should kill him, first, while he's distracted, but either because of the wound or the energy drawn in by the dogs, I can hardly move.

I've never really believed in the supernatural—apart from the whole invisible dog thing, of course—but I can feel something in this room, some force bigger than any of us, shifting position, battling for the upper hand. Or maybe it's the blood loss making me lightheaded.

Hutch is propped up against the wall. His eyes are closed, and his fists are clenched so hard the veins stand out on the backs. Is he somehow lending his energy to Kharon? It's ridiculous that I'm jealous of the connection he has with his dog. Hunter is my pal, my partner, but…Wait. Hunter is…the closest friend I've ever had. He's seen and heard everything. We have no secrets. I've never trained him the way Hutch has trained Kharon, because that's not what friends do.

"Hunter!" My mouth is dry. "Hunter…get'm."

His gaze never shifts from those other eyes, but an ear flicks and the tail gives a tiny wag.

I see a shimmer surround the two dogs, a white glow. Kharon looks smaller, now, and that head is just a dog's head, not a monster's. While Hunter…His stupid trench coat has fallen from his shoulders, his flat Lab fur is bristling and his ears are cocked. He looks more like a wolf than I've ever imagined he could.

I'm *helping*.

I'm assuming that's the right thing to do.

Hutch lets his breath out in a hiss, and Kharon's chest puffs out as the dog regains strength. Hutch is helping too. We can't have that. I push myself up on one arm, lunge forwards through dizzy waves, and punch him in the nose. It's not elegant, but it does the job. It's a punch for Phoebe Knight, Ann and Delphine, and for me and my dog. Hutch gasps, and Kharon breaks eye contact.

"No, no, no!" One hand on his nose, Hutch flaps the other at

Kharon. The big beast reacts as if it's been kicked, bows its head and shrinks into itself. And keeps shrinking. Hunter towers over the other dog with eyes like looking at the sun through a pinhole. Kharon whimpers, rolls over, tries to wriggle away on its back towards Hutch, who is looking at Kharon and at Hunter with astounded fury that changes to horror, then grief.

Neither human nor dog is paying any attention to anything except each other. Kharon wags feebly, pawing at Hutch's knee. Hutch shifts his hand, wanting to pat, to comfort. It's all wrong. Kharon should be easing Hutch's exit from the world, not the other way round. I guess that's what happens when you break the rules.

I slip a hand into my pocket and touch my phone. Home button, then the bottom left of the screen, where it says 'Emergency', then three stabs where the 9 will be. I've practised this, though I never thought I'd really use it. As I make my third press, so faintly I hope it registers, the big black dog folds in on itself, flattening to a black, burned stain on the carpet.

Hutch is running his fingers through the air where Kharon was. He's never been able to touch his dog, of course, but there's a vast difference between a space that contains an intangible black dog nobody else can see and a space that only used to contain one. He's not trying to kill me now, which is great, but pain shoots through me and I realise he doesn't need to.

The fire in Hunter's eyes isn't white hot any more. It's faded to a cosy pinkish red, like the bar of an electric fire, and I wonder how I could ever have been scared of that comforting, familiar glow.

"Hunter," I drop to my knees, and beckon him over. No wonder he looked sad earlier, when he told me it wasn't time. He knew the time was coming, and soon. But that's OK. It hurts a lot, and I want it to be over. I get it, now. Your black dog isn't the bringer of death I always feared under Hunter's daft, playful exterior. It's a familiar presence, revealed at the end so you'll have company while everything else fades away. And I want a piece of that. Hutch won't hurt anyone else. My work is done, though good luck to whoever has the job of trying to sort out what the hell happened in here.

I hope Hunter's next gig is a good one. He's a good boy.

Here, Hunter. From the cradle to the grave, Hunter. Till death do us part. Hunter...why won't you look at me?

I slide out of the hospital bed and walk over to the window, holding on to the furniture as I go. The doctors tell me I shouldn't be alive; I lost half my blood, my body shut down, brain too, but my heart just wouldn't stop beating, even when they turned the machines off.

It was a nurse who told me the other thing, how I burst from unconsciousness calling out and looking wildly around. It took three of them to tidy me back into bed and squirt in some drugs.

The ache inside me isn't from the wound, isn't from the needles and tubes and the harsh mixture of medicines. It's loss.

I didn't even see him go, but I knew, knew before I was even conscious. Hunter broke the rules by not helping me to my death, and now he's gone. I can only hope he's been reassigned —some other cute little baby, this one blissfully unaware of his presence—but for all I know he's the one who's ceased to exist, instead of me. For the first few days I kept expecting a new dog to pop up—a fluffy puppy, the mirror of my fantasy new life for Hunter—but nothing. Seems my black dog privileges have been revoked.

There's only one person who can know how this feels. Now we really do have something in common. But I can't, I won't, seek him out. I remember what he said about a strong will. If mine had been stronger, if I'd been a smarter, tougher person, could I have saved Hunter from vanishing out of existence? It's not *fair*—Hutch and Kharon broke the rules for years and got away with it, until we came along. All we did was set things right. We didn't deserve to have it go so wrong for us instead.

I wonder what will happen, at the end. I'm not stupid enough to imagine I'm going to live forever. Now there'll be no Hunter to lay his paw just above my hand, the closest he can get to touching, and send me on my way with compassion in his kind, wise eyes and jerky on his breath.

My room looks out across a square, with the river in the distance. I watch the people criss-crossing from one street to another, hurried or chilled, on business or just strolling. They're all reasonably decent people, probably. I've removed—I've helped to remove—a threat to the nice people, someone who'd cheat them out of their money and, when it suited him, take their lives. It's what I grew up wanting to do, and I should be pleased. But I can't help feeling that the whole lot of them aren't worth what I've lost.

The black dogs trot at their heels like second shadows: poodles and cockers, big Newfoundlands and tiny chihuahuas. Anything that comes in black, and plenty of mongrels, too. From up here, their eyes are tiny sparks. I flit from one to the next, hoping for the flap of a trench coat or the glint of sun off a pair of shades, but nothing. Following my own wishful thinking, he's beside some newborn's cot. I'll keep looking, Hunter, boy. I'll never stop.

All those people, and I'm the only one who knows that none of them is alone, or has to face the end alone. While I am, and I must.

10

WOLF'S HOLIDAY

On a mountain road, somewhere in Western Europe (the range of the grey wolf is wide), a woman was riding a motorcycle.

It was a trip she was supposed to take with her boyfriend, but he had dumped her two months previously. When she said she was going anyway it was obvious he didn't believe her, so she set out angry, but on this, the third morning of swooping curves and majestic views, she had stopped riding for him and was riding for herself.

The road climbed upwards, with forested slopes on one side and a drop to the valley on the other. There was no barrier, but a line of low markers painted white; sometimes the woman looked down between them and imagined what it would feel like to steer off the road and fall forever. But, for the most part, she kept her eyes on the vanishing point as she nudged the bike through the turns with her knees. The sun was bright, the air scented with sap and hot metal. She parked in a layby to eat the sandwich she'd bought seventy-five miles ago, but she felt all the time that she was being watched, and listened for rustles in the bushes over the tick-tock of the cooling engine.

She took a shorter break than she'd intended, straddled the bike, kicked up the sidestand, started the engine.

A wolf burst out of the undergrowth behind her.

She was too startled to do anything but gun the throttle, scattering gravel as she bumped back onto the road. When she looked in the mirror she saw that the wolf was chasing her, his paws smacking the hard asphalt one-two-three-four and his tongue drooling out like a dog's. If she accelerated the wolf dropped back but kept on running. She slowed to let him catch up a little, then she carried on. After a mile or so of this, the wolf all the time galloping behind with his ears back and his hazelnut eyes fixed on the bike, she pulled up and let the engine idle, and the wolf trotted straight over. He didn't scare her now, because she could see he was all out of huff and puff, so she called: "Hey, fella, what do you want?"

"I want to go for a ride," the wolf panted.

"Not without a helmet, you don't," she replied. "You're a protected species."

She rode to the nearest big town with a motorcycle store and bought an open face, to fit his muzzle, and she rode back, wondering all the time if two and a bit days of solitude should really be enough to send you crazy. But the wolf was still there, waiting for her. She rearranged her tent and luggage to make room for him on the pillion, helped him get his front legs into the sleeves of the spare jacket she'd brought in case hers got soaked, and buckled the helmet strap under his chin.

"Do wolves have names?" she asked.

"Sure we do," he replied.. "Mine is Rolls-in-Squirrel-Guts."

"I'll just call you Wolf," she told him. And they were off.

She barely felt the extra weight of the wolf, and he balanced well, wedged in by her bags and bedroll. She rode carefully at first, but when she was sure he wouldn't shift around or lean the wrong way she began to take the corners faster. Sometimes she could hear him on the back singing into the wind, and sometimes he laid his jaw on her shoulder to look at the road ahead, his whiskers tickling the bare skin between her helmet and her jacket collar.

They began to descend, the woman guiding the bike between the potholes and patches of gravel, and stopped at a picnic table by a field of sheep. She felt a little anxious about the wolf and the sheep, but tried not to show it as she asked him whether she should take him back now.

"I'd rather go on with you," he said, "if you don't mind."

"Don't you have a pack?" she asked.

"Don't you?" he countered, since he had often seen packs of bikers racing through his mountains.

"Not right now."

"Me neither. I'm a lone wolf!"

She reached out a hand, then, and stroked his neck. The fur there was soft, like an old fleece sweater.

"We can be a pack," the wolf said.

So they rode on, through villages with wooden churches and through forests of tall pines where the light and shade flickered across their visors. Some of the people in the cars they passed thought the wolf was a bundle of spare gear under a tarpaulin. Some, who got a closer look, pointed out the cute clever dog to each other, but most didn't notice anything at all.

She started looking for a campsite well before dark, and found one down a bumpy track in a little wood. The wolf sat watching as she pitched the tent and lit a fire. His outline in the forest dusk might have been frightening if his fur hadn't been all messed up from the helmet and jacket. When the fire burned down he lay next to it and shared her sausages. By the time the stars came out he was blinking and dozing with his head on his paws.

"Well, goodnight," she said.

She thought he'd want to stay outside the tent, under the moon, but he told her wolves sleep in dens, *duh*, and followed her through the flap. He lay down by the entrance with his front legs crossed. When she woke in the morning, he was draped over her feet and his tail was across her hand. They got up while it was still half-light so they could hit the road early. The woman ate a granola bar, and while she packed up their camp the wolf trotted off into the trees for his breakfast of small rodents.

Before the wolf, but after the boyfriend, it had been good to ride on her own. Now that she had company, and furthermore company that never told her which way to go or how fast she should be going, the riding was doubly good. It felt sweet to share the experience when birds of prey hovered beside them on the thermals, or when she overcooked a bend and scraped the pegs hauling the bike around it. They found their travelling rhythm, like the steady beat of a four-stroke: early starts and early sleeps, with a couple of hundred miles between. Often they stopped for the woman to take photos and the wolf to pee on things. That way, they both made memories. If there was roadkill she drank coffee from her flask while the wolf ate his fill, and if there was no roadkill she bought raw hamburgers from a supermarket. In the evenings, when his hazelnut eyes gleamed like topaz in the campfire light, the wolf and the woman talked over all they had seen and felt and smelled. The nights he spent curled against her bedroll. Sometimes, in her sleep, she'd reach out and grab a fold of his warm, furry skin.

One day when they woke and stretched, she said: "Wolf, my holiday's almost over. I have to take you back."

"Let's just carry on travelling," begged the wolf, drooping his ears and tail to show how sad he was. He pleaded with her to think of all the world they had yet to see, and said when they ran out of money for petrol she could find work waitressing or picking fruit until they had enough to continue.

She said that didn't sound like such a great deal to her, and how about him earning the money, as a talking wolf? Frankly, she told him, if that was the way things were going she'd rather work in her air-conditioned office and take a fortnight off twice a year without having to worry about her finances." The wolf reluctantly agreed, and they turned back east into the morning sun.

She took the motorway, as time was running short, with the wolf huddled down against the wind blast. As they drew close to the spot where she'd picked him up he didn't talk or sing, just nuzzled the salty gap at her neck with his nose. She parked up and put a puck under the sidestand, then for the last time she took the wolf's helmet and jacket off so he could jump down.

His four paws had barely touched earth when a smaller, brown wolf ran up and bit him in the flank. He cringed while the other wolf growled and nipped at his face, but he didn't try to defend himself, and as she watched, the woman knew that he had lied to her about being a lone wolf with no pack.

After a few minutes the growling and nipping stopped and both wolves put their tails up.

"This is my daughter, Smells-like-Carrion," her wolf said. "My mate died giving birth to our last litter and I went a little nuts. I thought if I left my pack behind and kept moving I could get away from it all, but just like you, I have to go back to my job. I'm sorry I tried to make you ride on forever."

"I wished I could," she said. "Maybe, if your daughter doesn't object, we could do it again next year? Wolves need holidays too."

The wolf looked at Smells-like-Carrion, who narrowed her eyes and gave a slow nod. "Can we go to Portugal?" he asked. "I have cousins there."

"Sure," she said, and tweaked his ear.

She rode off slowly, checking her mirror often to see the two heads with their pointed muzzles watching her out of sight. The bike felt too light, now, and her neck was cold.

The woman returned to the wolves' mountain every summer, because Christmas holidays are for family; but summer holidays are for mountains, motorbikes, and a wolf who was always ready to scramble up on her pillion. As the years rolled on, she sometimes had to give him a boost.

They rode high passes where snow could block the way even in June, and river valleys where the grapes grew in green rows. Once they loaded the bike on a little ferry to hop from island to island, beach after white sand beach with the sun so scorching she had to brush the wolf every night as he shed his fluffy undercoat. Because they chose lonely routes and quiet camp- sites, the woman saw things she wouldn't otherwise have seen, from little roadside shrines to families of badgers playing in the moonlight—and the wolf, of course, left his scent in more places than most wolves could even dream of.

They didn't discuss the past or future further than the things they had seen that day and the roads they would take on the next; the sights and the smells and the curves were enough, and neither of them cared to spoil the holiday by thinking about their day job, because who does? One year, though, when she brought the wolf home, Smells-like-Carrion was waiting to meet them. At her side was a big-pawed brown pup whose hazelnut eyes were fixed on the bike. The woman didn't ask questions, but when she came the next summer she had added a sidecar.

11
ONCE WE WERE MEERKATS

The suns were at their highest point when the alarm went off.

Some of us were on sentry duty, some minding the children in the nursery. The ones lucky enough to have their rest period during the hottest part of the day were sleeping or sunbathing. Most of us were digging and building.

We scrambled for the shelter of the underground complex, scooping up kids and the infirm as we went, while the sirens screeched.

Our leader quietened us down. She got hold of the sentry who'd raised the alarm and took him aside so he could give her a statement. The rest of us took stock of who had tagged in. There were two missing: a surveyor, out checking the area for the best place to extend our site, and one of the engineers, who'd been working on the irrigation system out near the fences.

The leader made a statement to the effect that it was probably a false alarm, and the missing just hadn't heard the siren. We were to carry on with our work, maintaining extra high vigilance just in case. But the rumours were already flying; it's impossible to keep a lid on anything around here. Some kind of monster—vast, stealthy, unseen—stalking around the outside of our walls and fences. Plenty of us had heard it or smelled it, now we came to think of it (the scent was meat and ice), but none of us could say what it looked like.

We already had sandbugs, pricklemouths and jumping snakes to contend with. We didn't need invisible monsters too. We were just trying to build a city.

Once we were meerkats. We've seen pictures in the database.

They made us human-sized, so we can build human-sized homes for them, and we lost our tails. We still have the fur that keeps us warm in the cold nights and cool in the heat of the day, with a dark mask to protect our eyes from the sun. We still have strong hands and nails designed for burrowing, even though we also have tools. We're still tough enough to deal with predators, and immune to some types of venom. We need little water, and we can eat almost anything. Most of all, we still look out for each other. That's how we survive.

We used to be *cute*.

Our missing two didn't come back, and search parties headed out to look for them. We returned with nothing to report: no prints, no scent, no sign of a struggle. We concluded that our surveyor and engineer had run off together; it happens sometimes that one or two of us decide to leave and start a new life according to their own rules. It's not exactly encouraged, but there's nothing any of us can do to prevent it, and perhaps it's best to be rid of any dissatisfied element. We wished them well and forgot about them. We were *busy*.

The city was behind schedule. The terrain was tricky, and we were having problems setting up the water supply. It was the diggers' fault. No! The engineers! No, the planners who'd picked the site!

The human ships had already left Earth, bound for their new colony, and even if we'd been able to get a message to them, they could not have turned back without a great deal of trouble and expense. We would have thousands of souls incoming, and not enough space and food for them. Or for us.

We worked extra shifts, and those of us usually assigned to other jobs pitched in with the building work. We often found ourselves working alone to put in extra time on a project, rather than sticking in the groups that kept us safe from attack. Ears and eyelids drooped. All of us were tired and all of us were preoccupied.

We were not as vigilant as we should have been.

Our nights were short, but black and cold. One cold, black night a bunch of our teenagers chose to sneak out beyond the fences, looking for a kind of cactus that some among us were always willing to swear got you high. When they didn't find one, they teased a sandbug out of its burrow and poked at it for a while, trying to flip it over with sticks while avoiding the stingers. It was while they were dancing around their prey, giggling and shrieking, that they noticed the starlight fade and the night become blacker. They fell silent and looked up to see a patch of darkness blotting out the line between sky and desert. Still shrieking and giggling at the adventure, they fled for the safety of home, where they found an unamused sentry waiting at the exit point they'd cut in the fence.

We thought they were just making up a story to slide out of the trouble they were in for breaking bounds. Then it was discovered that the gang was one teenager short.

We're designed to cope with hostile environments and predatory wildlife. Our whole purpose is to turn desert planets into human homes. But this was outside our scope and way beyond our skills.

The building work fell ever further behind. More of us were assigned to guard detail, but even so we worked with one eye on our current job and the other glancing over our shoulders for danger. We got jumpy, and we made mistakes that cost us precious time and materials to fix.

The kids who'd run away from the desert night and left their friend behind began to drift away from each other and the rest of us.

Arguments began between those of us who wanted to get on with the job and those who wanted to arm ourselves, the whole lot of us, and sweep the desert for monsters. Some of us wanted to pull out altogether. There's a protocol for when a planet reveals a hidden danger missed by the initial surveys. We'd never needed to activate it, nor had we heard of any crew who had. It's a serious matter.

The rest of us asked, what were we so afraid of? Ghosts? Stories? Funny smells? Kid stuff.

We were divided.

That never happens. Unity is in our genes. Sure, we have our spats and squabbles, but they don't last. In the worst case the leader has to knock a few heads together, or someone bops someone else on the nose, and it's all sweet again. Because we have purpose. Together.

We don't just blindly follow instructions. We might have a vast bank of plans to work from, but every planet is different, so we often need to improvise and substitute. Each city we create is unique, built in response to the particular problems and advantages of the landscape and climate.

Not all of us are solid muscle, built for labour and protection. We are architects, technicians and scientists. Some of us are record-keepers, adding to the sum of knowledge that our crew and others can draw from. Some of us describe ourselves as artists, or even visionaries.

We scientists and visionaries set to work on this new problem.

Our research and discussions led us to the conclusion that there was no such thing as the invisible. Just because we, ourselves, could not see something did not mean it couldn't be seen. So we adapted the goggles we use for night work to help us see beyond our usual range.

We argued over whether the aim of our exploration should be to investigate or to kill. Either way, we concluded, we would need to defend ourselves. Our sentries already had electrical weapons as well as firearms, and to these we added a type that used sound to disable and disorientate.

Some of us secretly fashioned our own armaments: knives and clubs, crude but reassuring. One of us made a helmet of wires to protect his brain from what he described as alien mind-rays, and we teased him without mercy.

Then we went hunting.

Split into groups, weapons on our shoulders, we divided the desert surrounding our base into squares and we patrolled.

Nothing.

We tried at different hours of the day and night. We looked for tracks, and for burrows where a large creature might lie low if it heard us coming. We lost one of our fighters to a jumping snake, but this, at least, was the kind of loss we could understand.

One of us had an idea. We had done our patrolling in groups, of course. The ones who were taken had been isolated, working remotely or left behind. What if someone tried going into the desert alone?

One of us kept their idea a secret, so as not to be prevented, and executed it privately. One of us walked out into the night weaponless, without a word of goodbye to friends or family, and sat atop a dune with the cold wind ruffling their fur, and waited for the unknown.

It came. It came as a rush of meat-scented air, and a distortion in the line of the horizon. The goggles showed a glowing blur, vast and wavering. A formless cloud without recognisable features like legs, eyes, or teeth.

One of us spread furred hands out wide to demonstrate a lack of weapons, and looked at the monster, and did not faint or run away.

The cloud moved forward and settled in the sand around the dune, filling each wind-carved hollow. One of us touched a soft nose to something less than solid, more than gas.

Our little kids were first to figure out there was something going on, and cluster around the fence. Then our teenagers slunk out of the shadows, trying to look as if they were there by accident and found the whole thing boring. The rest of us came in pairs or groups, looking for our young or our friends. We huddled up to the fence and peered over each other, passing our pairs of goggles around.

"I think you should come out here. All of you," one of us called.

We debated. Was it a trick? Had we lost another to a monster that was now puppeting one of us to lure the rest into its maw? We raised our voices, and some of us scuffled in the sand, pulling towards or away.

The leader ended it. She stepped forward to do her leader's duty, and we would not let her go alone. Our strongest and bravest went first, but the rest of us were not far behind. None of us intended the kids to come, of course, but they sneaked along anyway, dropping to all fours, skittering between our legs and racing through the fence before we could grab them.

We would confront the unknown for ourselves, and for our lost, and for our human employers when they arrived.

We swarmed the dune together and stood in a mass. Parents held children in their arms. The leader drew herself up tall, at the very front, as if she could shield us all. Nobody whispered or chattered. We were never this silent.

Our silence, our stillness or our concentration allowed it

in. We all took it in at once: the knowledge that the cloud creature was alone and dying on a world that no longer held life, and so could not sustain it by renewing its cells—until we came.

Now we had questions, and we yelled them all at once.

"One at a time," the leader called, but we drowned her out.

We became aware of shapes forming in the foggy cloud, and we craned forward. Those of us with goggles, and the youngest of us, could see most clearly.

Our missing. They lay curled up, eyes closed and unresponsive, but none of them looked hurt, and they were breathing. Some of us broke away to run down and hold them. Eyes blinked open.

These two are too old, and this one too young, we now knew. For what? we wondered. We'd seen movies. We'd scared each other, as kids, with stories of crews who'd ended up as exhibits in some alien zoo.

The answer sent ripples through our minds, and raised the fur on our spines. We felt the strained gaps between atoms barely held together and we knew what would become of this planet when the force could no longer hold.

I need one. I take one.

"No deal," the leader said. "We're family. We stick together." We heard her words, but we also felt them as the alien felt them, broken down into emotion and sensation. It was a new kind of togetherness.

We considered the offer. We did not bicker or fight. Each of us turned the thought around silently, each in our own mind.

This city we're building with such care isn't for us. It's for them.

Their eyes aren't as good as ours, so there are lights all along the tunnel walls and in the subterranean spaces. Really, they prefer to be above ground, in the sunshine, so as well as setting up the solar panels we have to pour a lot of time and resources into houses with air-conditioning for their elite, and into safely fenced parks and sports arenas.

When it's done at last, they arrive in ships and move in to their new world. Those ships then carry us to the next unclaimed planet, to start all over again. There's no place that we can call home. It's a life that most of us like, but it isn't for everyone.

One of us said: "I'll do it."

One of us was scooped up into that cloud, and felt the planet fade away. One of us had our mind enveloped by another.

Tell me, it said.

So I began my story.

1 2

REMEMBRANCE

Harry squeezed into the narrow shelter, curled his tail around his thigh, and sat down. His sergeant, Chander, who was eating something ghastly out of a mess-tin, flicked his ears but did not look up.

"What are you eating?" Harry asked, shaking the wet from his own ears. The rain that fell here might not drench like a monsoon, but it was cold and it seeped through his fur.

"Rat," Chander said, still chewing.

"You know what rats eat."

"The rats eat my comrades. I eat the rats. I fall. The rats eat me…" He rested the tin on his knee while he made a sacred and complicated gesture with his paws.

"Well, thank God I'm not religious," Harry said.

Chander grinned at that, revealing a row of long teeth. Harry sat beside him in the shelter, a short tunnel dug into the side of the trench, so the two canids were shoulder to shoulder. It kept them warm, at least. While Chander ate, Harry removed his shirt and began the tricky business of burning the lice from the seams with a candle. He'd comb his fur later, before he slept, and perhaps enjoy a few precious hours free of itching before the bloody things bred again.

Harry smelled the approaching officer before he heard him, and pulled his shirt back on, hiding the broad black stripe down his back that differentiated his species from the other Greater Canids. He and Chander scrambled upright, bushy tails swinging for balance.

"Lieutenant. Sergeant." Captain Salt waved them back down. He had very blue eyes, and freckles that made him look, even to inhuman eyes, younger than he was. Despite his innocent appearance, he had a decade's service behind him. Salt was all right. An old Indian hand, he had commanded a canid company before. He had even bothered to work out that his lieutenant's name was Ari, not 'Arry, but by then the mistake was so ubiquitous that it had stuck.

"Your presence is requested for the wiring party tonight. Report to me at dusk."

"With that lot?" Chander asked, jerking his muzzle downwind to where their neighbours, a Tommy battalion, were posted. Harry and Chander's kind had been eradicated across this whole continent by the late Middle Ages, and the Tommies and *poilus* were, Harry sometimes thought, more frightened of the canids than they were of the Germans.

"Yes, with that lot. And behave yourself. I know your idea of a joke and it could get you shot."

"We don't need them to hold our paws! We can manage a little cutting job!" Chander protested.

"No doubt," Salt said, diplomatically. He reached out to give Chander a soft tap on the underside of his jaw; something else he had learned in his previous command. Chander lowered his large ears.

"You have no idea how many conferences and arguments in Whitehall it took to bring you into this war," the Captain said. "We could have had the whole lot over and done with by now if we'd had you from the start, in my opinion. But someone had to decide whether it was sporting to turn you loose on the Germans, and vouch that you wouldn't eat your allies. So don't mess about," he finished, raising his voice to its usual level and giving his usual smile.

"You need me and my ears, don't you?" Chander smirked.

"And Harry and his brain," the Captain told him. "Between the pair of you, you just about make up a half decent soldier. Good grief, Chander, you might have cut the tail off," he finished, and was gone.

Chander, stretching himself out as long as he could in the confined space, pulled a crumpled pack of cigarettes from his pocket, lit one, and stuck it in the side of his mouth.

"What are you doing? What about your nose?" Harry wrinkled up his muzzle.

Cigarettes, like chocolate, arrived in their rations, and were kept to trade with those Tommies brave enough to venture along the Lines to where the Queen's Own Jackalmen were posted. So much of what they were given was useless, or almost useless—like the gas masks, meant for a flat and snub-nosed face, or the helmets that squashed their ears uncomfortably. They couldn't wear the boots, and had to improvise canvas coverings for their feet when the trenches were wet, as they usually were.

Chander took a defiant puff. "Listen, Lieutenant, the less I smell around here the better."

"You won't catch many rats like that."

"I can still hear them, can't I? Best ears in the company, me. And not smelling them makes them easier to eat."

Harry shook his head. "What you need," he said, "is vegetables. We've got a couple of hours. I'm going to see if I can scrounge some cabbages."

"The French villagers will shoot you like a fox in the henhouse. They'll think you're after their babies."

"And *that's* why you shouldn't eat rats in front of the humans."

"Old Salty doesn't count," Chander said, swallowing the last of his meal. "Shall I catch you one while you're out?"

"No thanks." Harry wriggled out of the shelter and brushed the mud from his tail.

"I'll get some kip, then. Them badgers down below kept me awake again earlier."

"You can't hear badgers. Don't show off." Harry slung his gas mask and kit over his shoulder.

"Remember!" Chander called after him. "You don't ask for cabbages—you ask for shoes!"

"Shoes." Harry shook his head and padded off along the slippery duckboards. Chander was already lying back, eyes shut and whiskers twitching as he dozed.

"*Choux*," Harry said. He smiled what he thought of as his European smile, the one where his lips stayed over his teeth. Peasants like this woman had never seen anyone like him outside a circus or travelling exhibition, and he wanted her to help him as a favour, not out of fear.

The young woman in the doorway looked silently up at him. Harry was tall, and his large ears heightened the effect. He had quickly learned to stoop—except around officers, who would snap at him to stand up straight and not slouch, man...or dog or whatever you are! He dropped into a crouch in the barnyard, lowered his ears, and swung his tail up onto his knee. Europeans seemed to like tails.

This farm behind the lines had little left. The cavalry had taken the horse, and a shell had taken the barn. The crops had been trampled by marching feet, and most of the hens scared out of laying by the sound of bombs. Harry noted each new privation and hole, and felt it as though the farm, his discovery of two weeks ago, was his own property.

He didn't like to beg, but they simply had to supplement the daily ration with an occasional fresh egg, or a rabbit, or something green. Corned beef and biscuit wasn't enough to keep eyes, ears and teeth sharp.

Finally, the woman said something rapid in French that was far beyond Harry's skills. It sounded like a question, and he thought he made out the word '*bébé*'.

"No!" Harry said at once, shaking his head so his ears flapped. His paws made quick movements of denial, almost like one of Chander's religious gestures. The woman frowned and went back inside, but the door stayed open. Harry waited. Just because she hadn't shot him yet, didn't mean today wasn't the day.

Perhaps he should have sent Chander, who seemed to get on better with people the less effort he made. He ate rats, bared his fangs, and claimed to hear things he couldn't possibly hear, yet they liked him. Harry tried so hard to fit in, and was shunned. But it was restful to see someone out of uniform, getting on with their ordinary life as best they could. The houses here, the clothes, the faces and voices, were memories he wanted to take home with him, despite the stares and the risks.

The woman returned with a small sack. It smelled of corn, but also of cabbages, and he felt two firm, round lumps inside.

He should offer something in return. He tried, every time he came, but was always refused. Maybe she just didn't understand.

"*Je*...aid?" he said, and mimed chopping firewood with an axe.

The woman shook her head decisively. Maybe he should have acted out something less violent.

"*Merci, madame! Merci beaucoup!*" With another European smile, Harry took the sack and walked away.

His return journey took him through the reserve trenches

and the support line. Soldiers loafed, or wrote, or cooked meals only slightly less awful-smelling than Chander's. Some were too tired to pay attention as Harry walked past, while others gave him the familiar, silent stare. One gripped the collar of a little terrier, which fixed bright eyes on Harry and bristled all the way along its back. Its tail was wagging, at least, which made it the friendliest creature Harry had met since leaving his own company.

When he had first arrived, Harry had tried saying "Good morning!" and "Hello!" as he passed through the trenches. He still called out greetings as he moved along, but he no longer hoped to get an answer. He spoke because if he spoke, and spoke English, he was less likely to find himself bayonetted by his own side.

"What you got there, then? Is it a baby?"

"Baby-eater! Let's see!"

Neither of the two boys standing in front of him reached up to Harry's chest, and he was amazed they had passed the physical exam. That was the trouble, he thought—most Tommies hadn't been born into a warrior caste, but grabbed for the Front from all sorts of jobs. Teachers; factory workers; coal miners, though most of those worked as sappers, not soldiers. No wonder they had no sense of who and what Harry was.

"No, look," he said. "Cabbages! Just cabbages!"

He rolled one out to show him, and the boy snatched it from his paw. His ears, Harry noticed, stuck straight out, and were very pink.

"Dogs don't eat cabbages!" he said. Harry, torn between *Yes, they do* and *We're not dogs*, said nothing.

He said nothing when the boy and his friend began kicking his cabbage back and forth like a football, scattering greenish leaves. He said nothing when they jostled close to him, smelling of sweat and dirt, grabbing his paws to examine the pads and the claws. He only moved away when one of them tried to snatch a button from his coat. That was what you did to dead Germans, not living allies.

"Go on," the boy pleaded. "Give us one. Souvenir."

If he had been a boy himself, Harry could have taunted and shoved back, but his strength and teeth were too dangerous. No matter how much he was provoked, retaliation was strictly forbidden. He couldn't even growl.

He took cigarettes from his coat, two packs, three, as many as he had stuffed in there thinking they would come in useful, and thrust them into the outstretched, grubby hands. Like street children at home, he thought. But street children could be dispersed with a snap of teeth and a few curse words, all the while knowing they were in no danger and laughing back at him.

Harry returned to his own trench with one cabbage, no cigarettes, and an intact uniform. He decided this counted as an overall victory. Certainly the London newspapers would have painted it that way.

"Chander, I know you're proud of your lugholes, but lay them flat before you get them blown off, will you?" Captain Salt said in an undertone. Obediently, the sergeant folded his ears back against his skull.

There were six of them in the party: Harry, Chander, the Captain, and three Tommy lads. They crouched around Salt and studied the map on his knees, which showed their theoretical journey to a circled target in neat pencil lines with arrows.

Salt hadn't drawn a route back. Return journeys tended to be hurried and disorderly, if they were made at all.

"Learn to trust Chander's ears," Salt told the three strangers. "A lot of nonsense might come out of his mouth, but he's pretty useful when he shuts up and listens."

One of the boys gave a quiet, nervous laugh.

"I can hear the badgers scratching down in the earth," Chander said, swivelling his ears to demonstrate. For dramatic effect, he swivelled his eyes, too, and gestured with his paws.

"No, he can't," sighed Harry.

"I can! They keep me awake!"

Harry nudged him hard in the ribs, and he subsided. They were strange and foreign enough already, without his sergeant giving them supernatural powers on top.

"We'll be cutting the wire in front of the enemy positions here and here," Salt's pink finger stroked the map.

"Why?" Chander asked. Harry showed him a flash of teeth, quick enough for the humans to miss it in the dark, but the captain didn't seem upset by this insubordination.

Salt let Chander get away with murder, and Salt outranked Harry, but Harry was directly responsible for keeping Chander in line. The captain was not making this job any easier.

"You don't need me to tell you there's a big push coming," Salt said. "Our sappers have been tunnelling under the enemy's position to set mines. Tomorrow the whole lot goes sky high, and we mop up whatever's left."

Harry imagined the soldiers toiling in the dark, the yawning space beneath the trench, and the explosion underground that would kill, maim or simply bury alive. He rolled his shoulders forward so his neck disappeared into its ruff of fur, and shifted his bare feet for the reassurance of solid earth beneath them.

"Any more questions? Good. Let's go."

Harry was careful to keep his ears tucked back as he climbed the ladder and emerged from the trench. The landscape, with its craters, tracks and occasional blasted trees, bore little resemblance to Salt's map. Harry stared out across No Man's Land, trying to align the landmarks he could make out with his memory of the terrain. The wind ruffled the fur of his neck, in the gap between jacket and helmet. It almost always blew towards the enemy lines, making him feel exposed. But there was nobody on the other side to smell him; the enemy held no territory where any of the Greater Canids could be conscripted or recruited.

Cutting the enemy's barbed wire meant an attack was coming within the next few days. Parties like this one went out, night after night, to repair their own wire and cut the other side's. Give your soldiers a clear passage to the enemy, and block the enemy's path to you. Like a game.

To reach the enemy wire, they first had to navigate their own. Harry stooped, crouched and lifted, losing a tuft of fur from his neck on one of the barbs. Chander moved up beside him, gliding along the ground with a boneless crawl that even Harry found unnerving.

"Bleeding," he observed, and put his tongue to Harry's neck to staunch the blood and cover its sharp scent. Harry pulled away. Soldiers didn't do that; not in Europe.

"No time," he justified himself to Chander's hurt expression. "Just a scratch."

"You must feel at home here, eh, Wolfy?" one of the boys whispered. He smelled of shaving. "Seeing as it's No *Man*'s Land. Get it?"

"Quiet, Jones," Salt said, adding "I imagine he's heard that one, lad."

Harry had, but he was grateful the boy had even spoken to him.

A star shell exploded above them, flooding the field with light. Harry shut his eyes to prevent the reflective glow that could give their position away. When he opened them, Salt and the lads, who had flattened themselves to the ground beside him, were lying still to rub their eyes. Harry couldn't see perfectly, but his sight worked better in the dark than theirs, and he could use his nose, too. Salt made a slight movement with his hand, urging Harry into the lead.

He moved one limb after the other, pausing to listen as each paw set. He disliked going on all fours, because it looked too doglike, but here both canid and human must crawl or die. Big guns were firing in the distance, and the vibration trembled his whiskers. Somewhere an owl called, because not far away there were woods and fields still whole, with small creatures to hunt. His nose told him the sudden rustle to his left was only a rat, but Salt and the soldiers all froze at the sound. He beckoned them on, and the procession continued its slow passage to the wire.

A single shot. The kind a bored sentry fires into the night.

After all the stillness and the listening, the noise shocked Harry into a bare-fanged growl. Jones—the one who had made the No Man's Land joke—paused on hands and knees, then sank forward and down. Harry covered the ground in a moment to crouch at his side, though he had smelled the brain mixed in with his blood and knew there was little hope, but one of the others shoved him back.

"Get away from him!" he shrieked.

So much for silence. Harry went sprawling, and another bullet whined over his head. With Chander close behind, he slithered into the slight depression where a shell had landed. Cold, muddy water soaked through his uniform to his belly and thighs, but he was only interested in keeping skin and flesh intact.

There were more shots, then silence. Whoever had been firing obviously thought they'd hit their target. Harry poked his muzzle over the lip of the crater, and sniffed. Salt and the others were both still alive, at least. He let out a low bark, designed to reach as far as Salt's ears but not the enemy trench beyond. One of the soldiers flopped into the hole, then the captain joined them, half-dragging the other. The five lay awkwardly huddled together. The boy who had shouted at Harry lifted his head to see where his friend lay, and Salt pushed it back down.

"He's dead, lad. Harry, tell him."

"It's true." Harry didn't elaborate, because what good would it do the boy to know that a canid nose could tell living from dead at this distance, or that Chander's ears were keen enough to pick up even faint, shallow breaths? Chander had found a wounded officer that way, saved his life, but Harry had told him to say he'd stumbled across the casualty by accident.

"So. Jerry's woken up," Salt said, "but that wire needs cutting tonight."

Neither Tommy spoke. It was left to Harry, the eater of babies and now, apparently, bodies, to take the lead. He constructed a European smile: cheerful, but not too cheerful, acknowledging the loss of Jones. There was no reaction. They couldn't see him, of course.

"We'll cut it, sir," he said.

"*À l'attaque*, then!" With these words, Salt scrambled back out of the hole.

"I don't know any French," Chander protested, staying still. Harry gave him a shove. The Tommies just stared, and Harry couldn't resist showing off to them. He'd bet they didn't know any French themselves, while Harry shared that gift with the officer. The *other* officer, he reminded himself, although the lowliest Tommy lieutenant held authority over the highest-ranked canid.

"Yes, you do. What about 'souvenir', like all those bits and bobs you pinch when we take an enemy trench, or pick up in the villages? That's French. It means a memento, a remembrance." He eyed his sergeant. "You don't know what those words mean, either, do you?"

Chander shrugged, and swiped Harry's face with his tail as he crawled after the captain.

The wires sprang apart under Harry's cutters. To him, the click of the blades carried like a shot, and the uncoiling metal sang. He used his coat to muffle the sounds, but he couldn't cover the heavy breathing of the two lads. Salt crouched, holding his pistol, and Chander had his head close to the wire, clipping away with apparent enjoyment.

Harry placed his paw on Chander's shoulder and his muzzle to his ear.

"You're supposed to be listening out," he mouthed into the furry triangle. Chander flicked his ear away.

"Doing both," he growled under his breath.

Harry was still deciding how to respond to that when the German soldier loomed out of the night beside him.

The wind—the bloody prejudiced wind that always blew towards the enemy—had betrayed their ears and noses, or they had got distracted. Whether the grey-clad soldier had been out on a wiring party of his own, was returning from some other mission or had simply got lost, he had not expected to find two canids in his way. His eyes opened very wide, and he drew breath for the shout that would bring the enemy up and out and upon them. But before he could make a sound, Harry's fangs were clamped around his throat.

Harry twisted as they fell, so the corpse was cushioned by his lithe, soft body. Then he rolled out from under it and spat away his mouthful of chewed flesh. Panting, wide-jawed, he plunged his muzzle into the filthy water of a shell-hole to rinse it, catching a brief reflection of his wild, yellow eyes and bloody maw. The other four watched him rise to his knees. Salt still held his gun at the ready, and Harry wasn't entirely sure who for. He shook himself, and glared at the terrified Tommies, daring them to speak.

Captain Salt rolled the body over with his foot, concealing the gaping wound at the throat, and kicked it away so the head was submerged in the shell-hole. He gestured with his pistol, back the way they had come.

Silently, rapidly, they made their way across No Man's Land, through their own barbed wire defences and down into the trench. The two surviving Tommies turned towards their station without saying a word.

"Goodnight," Salt called after them. To Harry, who knew Salt well, his voice had a hard edge.

"Goodnight, sir," one of the boys replied, and added, after a hesitation, "All right, Wolfy."

"See you, Wolfy," muttered the other.

They moved off down the trench with the sloped backs and dragging feet of the utterly weary.

"It's a strong word, 'atrocity,'" Salt said, "but if they bring in that body, they'll use it."

"Why is it different from using a bayonet? Or a gun, come to that?" It was more honest, to kill with the teeth, and tidier than scattering brains everywhere the way the bullet had done to Jones.

"It's not, Harry, and I know that as well as you do. But the people at home won't. Still, can't be helped now. Very prompt action. Well done."

"Think they'll talk?" Chander asked, looking past Salt into the blackness where the Tommies had disappeared.

"No. If I did, I'd have shot them both. Night." Salt jerked his arm in a half-hearted salute and left for his dugout, which was, by trench standards, first class accommodation.

Harry leaned back against the wall and looked upwards, to where the sky was lightening. He folded his paws in his lap and let his eyes close.

"I saved everyone's lives," he said.

"Maybe you'll get a medal," Chander yawned. "That'll be nice."

"There was no time to do anything else, and a shot would have been noisy."

Chander's only answer was another yawn.

"We're all just 'Wolfy' to them," Harry continued.

"They're mostly all just Tommy to us."

He heard the scrape and hiss as Chander lit a match, concealing the spark behind cupped paws. The burning tobacco reached his nose a few moments later, along with the noise of slow, contented breaths.

"I hope those badgers don't keep me awake again," Chander mumbled. "There's a whole family of them. All scratching away."

"Shut up." Harry wriggled his shoulders, trying to find a comfortable resting place for them against the muddy earth. The regular wheeze of Chander's breath told him that the sergeant had dropped off already, but Harry could not. His muscles refused to relax, and his feet twitched in the mud. His closed eyelids acted as a cinema screen for endless footage of soldiers crawling, soldiers shooting, soldiers falling. He drifted close to the edge of sleep, only for a frame of his mental movie to startle him back into half-consciousness with a jerk of paw or knee. In sepia shades of mud, he watched stooped men tunnelling underground. Digging. Burrowing. *Scratching.*

"Chander!"

The sergeant's eyes snapped open. He was too well-trained to move until he knew where he was—many a soldier had sleepily risen and stretched, only to be picked off by a sniper—but the fur visible on his neck and tail fluffed up, settling slowly as he glared at Harry.

"Get out of the way. I want to listen to your badgers."

Ruffled and with one ear inside-out, Chander looked as if he wanted to argue, but when he saw Harry's expression he closed his muzzle with a click.

Harry placed his head exactly where Chander's had been, and tilted his ears back. His sense of hearing might not be as acute as the sergeant's, but as he held his breath he could make out a faint scratching, far below. He sat back upright.

"Tell Captain Salt I need to see him," he said. "Now."

———

"*Oeufs*," Harry said. "Please?"

From the look the woman gave him, he thought he must have got the wrong word and asked for pineapples, or top hats. She held up one finger and disappeared into the farmhouse.

He had left Chander sitting in the shelter like a king, holding court as a stream of visitors from their own and the neighbouring companies dropped by to congratulate and thank him.

Nobody else could have heard the enemy miners beneath their position, let alone pinpointed their precise depth and the direction of their digging. That had enabled the British sappers to dig into the tunnel and lay an explosive charge. Harry and Chander had felt it under their feet as they sat side by side in the shelter, Harry teaching Chander the French words for his favourite foods.

The Tommies had started touching Chander's ears, as a good luck charm. He bore it patiently, and had even begun to give away his cigarettes rather than smoking them. He'd been offered gifts himself, of course, and politely refused the inappropriate ones.

"We don't eat chocolate," he explained, and got respectful nods and apologies.

Not every soldier who came to marvel at Chander stopped to talk to Harry, or the others in his unit. But enough did that they had begun to make friends, and to teach each other card games. The boy with the sticking-out ears had come; he hadn't recognised Harry, but he had persuaded a couple of the canid privates to play football with him. With a proper, leather ball.

Chander had offered to come to the farmhouse today, try

out his new language skills, but Harry wanted to see the farmer's wife again. Still waiting on the step, he was uncomfortably aware that farmers kept guns, for shooting foxes. But when the woman returned, she carried a baby in her arms. It was barefoot, like Harry, and kicking as much as it could manage through several layers of frilly clothing.

"I really don't eat..." Harry was beginning, when the baby was placed in his arms. He cradled it uncertainly while the mother watched, all smiles. Its clean scents of soap and powder, and its softness, were so unlike anything he experienced in the trenches that he rested his chin on its head to breathe it in.

The woman held up her finger again, and went back inside. Harry, not sure what was expected of him, jiggled the baby, who reached up to grab a handful of the soft fur spilling over his shirt collar. Since nobody was watching, he licked the baby's ear, small, curved and bare.

This time, when she returned, the woman was holding a box camera. Still smiling, she raised it to her face.

"*Souvenir,*" she said.

Harry's ears flicked at the word, but he didn't mind it when it came with a smile and was requested, not grabbed. He was part of the strangeness of the times she lived in; a part she valued and wanted to preserve. There were surely many she would rather forget. Harry guessed he had become the Frenchwoman's canid, as she was *his* farmer's wife.

She cooed to the baby, to attract its attention. It turned at the sound, and its fist tightened in Harry's fur.

The baby had no teeth, and no comprehension of how to smile for the camera anyway, but Harry showed every one of his.

GERBIL 07

"Good morning, James!"

That meant the Old Man had a mission for me. I sat up and ran a paw through my whiskers.

"Morning, Old Man. Gerbil-O-Seven reporting, ready once again to save the world and get the girl. What's the deal?"

"I do wish you wouldn't call me that."

"Why not? In gerbil years, you're eight hundred."

He reached to open the cage door. I bounced out into his hand.

"Whatever it is, Old Man, I'm ready. I've fully recovered from my last mission and I'm at my physical peak. I've been clocking two hundred RPM in the wheel and my teeth can gnaw through a quarter-inch steel hawser. Psychologically, I'm up for any kind of physical or mental torture the bad guys can think of. Women want me. Men want to throw things at me." I drummed my hind feet. "Bring it on."

"I need you to plant a listening device in the gents' toilets at the Swedish Embassy."

"Oh." I tried to keep the disappointment out of my voice. "Wily old Swedes up to their tricks again, eh? I always say you can never trust a Swede. Never fear, they shan't take over the world as long as I'm around to stop them. And their women are gorgeous."

The Old Man's hand closed around me, and I found myself lifted until I was on a level with his eyes. I squeaked.

"James, listen carefully," he said. "You are not a Double O agent. You do not have a licence to kill. You—are—a—gerbil. A genetically engineered surveillance tool. You carry tiny cameras. You plant tiny bugs. The backchat is an unexpected—and unwanted—side effect." He tapped my nose gently with his finger. "You don't drink martinis—you nearly drowned last time. Also, for your information, you're a girl."

"But my name's James!"

"Do you have any idea how hard it is to sex a two-day-old gerbil?"

"I'm Gerbil-O-Seven!"

"You're the seventh prototype in the series."

"What happened to prototypes one through six?"

"You don't want to know."

I blinked one eye, then the other. "May I ask a question?"

"Sure," he said, more gently. His hands were warm and steady.

"Why am I a gerbil?"

"Biologically, religiously, or philosophically speaking?"

"I mean, I'm kind of noticeable. Why not a rat, or a mouse?"

"Because their little naked feet freak me out, OK? Now get some sleep before your mission, and remember: you do not save the world. You do not stop and sit up in the middle of running for your life in order to make wisecracks. You just do the job you were created for."

As he placed me back in the cage, he added, more softly, "And stay safe. You silly little thing."

I curled my tail around my nose and moodily examined my

hindpaws, with their dark nails and delicate fuzz of fine hair—
the cause, apparently, of my existence as me.

Thanks, feet. Thanks a whole bunch.

———

The Old Man helped me into my webbing harness, loaded up
with a selection of miniature survival tools.

"Now, because this is a delicate mission, you're going to be
briefed by a specialist first," he told me. "Want me to carry you,
or would you rather go in your little ball?"

"I'll drive, thanks."

The ball gave me time to think. Well, I was pedalling frantically to keep up with the Old Man, but the translucent red
plastic kept me isolated with my thoughts. I took a corner at
speed, doing a little jump and leaning hard right, and absent-
mindedly ground my teeth. A delicate mission. Something only
I could handle. My chance to redeem myself in the Old Man's
eyes after the Mornington Crescent mix-up and what had
become known as the Senior Officers' Biscuit Tin Snafu. But
what was it?

I rolled out of the lift and followed the Old Man down a
corridor. He stopped, knocked, and held the door open for me. I
like to make an impressive entrance, so I drove full pelt into a
filing-cabinet. The ball separated into its two halves on impact,
and I hopped out at a pair of feet. Female, from the nail polish.

"Oh my God, look at his little harness! He's adorable!"

I flashed the Old Man a look. It said: *See? Women want me.*

He flashed me one back. It said: *Please don't say that out loud.*

"He's a she, actually. James, this is Marta Harris."

"Hi." I stretched a little taller and allowed my whiskers to
tremble in that irresistible way of mine. Marta crouched down
and laid her hand flat on the carpet, palm up. When I jumped

on, she curled her other hand over me as she slowly raised me to her desk.

I like a woman who knows how to handle a gerbil.

"Can I, er, get you a pencil to chew, or anything?"

"No thanks, I'm on duty."

"All right." She released me, and lowered her chair so I was level with her face. "Now, listen carefully. We have reason to believe that there's a mole in the Belgian embassy, feeding sensitive information to hostile powers."

"Swedish embassy," I corrected, to show I was on the ball.

"The Belgians are working out of the Swedish embassy at the moment while they have some repairs done to theirs."

Swedes *and* Belgians... The plot thickened!

"You'll plant your bug, and if our Belgian tries to pass information to his contact, we'll have him. Let's attach this to your harness."

She clipped the listening device to the strap over my chest, where I could remove it easily. It was about the size of a sunflower seed, and painted in black and white stripes to match. If anyone saw me, I'd just be a gerbil holding a treat. While wearing a harness. In the middle of the Swedish Embassy.

"That should be all the equipment you need," she said.

"What about a suicide pill? In case I get captured?"

"Don't tempt me," said the Old Man. "You're not going to get captured. If you are, all you have to do is keep your mouth shut so they don't know you can talk. Can you manage that?"

"I suppose so." I shuffled my hind paws.

"I can find you some rat poison if it would make you feel better. Now, anything else before we take you over there?"

I twitched my whiskers. "Just one thing. You say there's a mole in the Swedish Embassy. Well, pretty soon there's going to be a..."

My quip was stifled by his hand as he scooped me off Marta's desk.

So far, it had been a run-of-the-mill mission. I scampered through the embassy door using a crisp packet as cover, hitched a ride on a briefcase to the third floor, then followed my nose to the gents', using the pattern on the carpet as camouflage. It was pretty nice, as washrooms go. Light poured through a floor-to-ceiling window of what I hoped was one-way glass. Soap and moisturiser in glass bottles. A pile of soft, white towels; I had a quick bounce on them before getting down to business.

"An absolutely textbook infiltration," I narrated to myself, running a paw through the fur between my ears. "Now, where to plant my device?"

The embassy was swept for bugs regularly, but until that happened I had to conceal it from casual inspection. Fortunately, gerbils can get places larger secret agents can't. I swarmed up the pedestal of one of the basins, and fixed the device among the downflow pipes under the curve of the sink. There! No other field operative could have done that. Not even one with really tiny fingers.

I was pretty dusty and cobwebby by this time. Fortunately, I was in the perfect place to clean up. I hopped over to the mirror. I could only see the tops of my ears, but they were looking good. I was pretty sure I was raffish. And rakish. Roguish, even. A loveable scoundrel breaking hearts in the name of my country. I allowed myself to drift into a daydream.

"For your courage and intelligence in the field, and for saving the world, I name thee Dame James of the British Empire," said the Queen, and she lowered the ceremonial sword.

The creak of the door opening snapped me out of it. I barely had time to squeeze myself behind the soap bottle before two men entered. My heart was going at double its usual speed; I calculated it at approximately 800 beats per minute. Could this be my mole and his contact?

To my excitement, they began to exchange coded signals. They leaned in close to each other, and one man wrapped his arms around the other man's back, slipping both thumbs under his belt. Obviously passing information.

And then...

They *made contact!*

I had never actually seen anyone make contact before, but what else could it be when one human's mouth touched another?

The two of them spent a good five minutes passing information while I watched, fascinated. It must have taken a great deal of work to come up with a code as fiendishly complicated as this one. And my listening device would be sending it all straight back to the Old Man....if only they were talking, instead of sort of sighing and moaning. Good job I'd stuck around to provide an eyewitness account!

As they separated, tidying hair and straightening ties, I leaned forward to get a better look at their faces.The bottle of soap toppled into the sink, and smashed.

I froze.

"Hell!" the taller, blonder man swore, in Swedish. Did I mention that fluent Swedish is among the many talents at my disposal?

"A little rat! Or a big mouse!" he continued, making a grab for me.

No time to congratulate myself on my linguistic prowess. I took a flying leap from the sink, spreading my limbs for distance and twirling my tail for control. (All standard gerbil equipment, by the way.) I wasn't prepared for one of the Swedes to take a flying leap of his own and snatch me out of the air. I tried to sink my teeth into his thumb, but he had me round the middle and I couldn't reach. He brought me level with his face.

"I think this is a gerbil, Lars."

"I don't care if it's a lemming, Jens! Kill the tiny pervert!"

"How dare you!" I struggled. "I'm in service to Her Majesty the Queen!"

Oops. I wasn't supposed to let on that I could talk. Especially in Swedish.

They stared at me.

I stared at them.

I remembered that if one of them was my mole, he'd be Belgian, not Swedish.

I realised this was the least of my problems.

"If Her Majesty the Queen saw you she'd jump on a chair and scream," said the first Swede, eventually.

"I very much doubt that," said the second. "The Queen looks like a pretty tough old lady to me."

"OK, talking gerbil," said the Swede with his hand round me. "I'm going to open my hand. Don't jump, please. Or bite."

"Give me one good reason why I shouldn't."

"Because you're interesting and I want to look at you. Besides, you'll break a leg or something."

"Fair enough."

He opened his hand and I stood on the palm.

"Hey, you have a little harness! And tiny small miniature tools! Look, Lars, he's got a whole spy kit here!"

I tensed. If he carried on exposing my secrets like this, I was going to have to kill them both. Somehow.

"Everything you say to me is going straight to my headquarters," I told him. "They'll come after you if you hurt me. I'm very valuable."

"I just bet you are." He cupped his other hand behind me on

his palm. "And what is a little small valuable spy guy like you doing in here?"

I considered my options. If he knew I was onto him, he might get desperate. Or I might be able to blackmail him in return for my life.

"I'm here to catch a mole. I saw you make contact and pass information to each other, and my boss heard the whole thing through the bug I planted. Kill me and there's nowhere you can hide. Be reasonable, and you'll be out in a couple of years."

I was prepared for whatever reaction came—except, as it turned out, both Swedes roaring with hysterical laughter.

"Nobody here is a mole, little spy gerbil," said Jens. He'd held me securely as he shook with mirth, and I was grateful, if a little seasick. "We were just...oh my Lord God, how old are you actually?"

"Eight months. And a week." I didn't mention the girl thing. Some people are weird about that, as if my being an entire different species was somehow less relevant.

"Let's just leave it as passing information, then." Jens decided. "But not to any enemies. OK? Would you like a biscuit? I have one in my pocket from the World Hunger summit this morning."

A biscuit? I stiffened. Was he telling me he knew about the Snafu, and my disgrace? Was this blackmail? On the other hand —I sniffed—he *did* have a biscuit on him.

Suddenly the door burst open, and a man with dark hair and wild eyes ran through. When he saw us, he pulled out a Walther P99; compact anti stress version, with the suppressor kit.

"Hands up!" he snarled. Both Jens and Lars obeyed, and I found myself raised into the air and held high above the hard, tiled floor.

This mission was putting whole weeks on my life. Months, even.

The gunman kicked the door shut behind him.

"You two are my hostages," he informed us as he kicked the door shut.

"We *three*," I squeaked. He didn't seem to hear.

"Hey, spy gerbil," Jens said out of the corner of his mouth. "Run down my sleeve."

"What?"

"Maybe you can save yourself."

I nodded, though he was carefully looking straight ahead, and dived down the sleeve of his jacket. He had nice cufflinks, I noticed. And hairy wrists. I passed the armpit and carefully scrabbled down inside his shirt.

"It's not funny!" snapped the gunman, just as I squeezed past the waistband of Jens's trousers. I must have been tickling him, but there was nothing I could do about it. I shinned down his shin and poked my head out of his trouser cuff.

Jens wanted me to get away, but I wasn't leaving my Swedish mole and his companion to die. They'd been pretty kind to me, and besides, I wanted the glory of their capture for myself. Using Jens's shoe as a mirror, I worked out the lie of the land. The gunman had edged my Swedish companions over to the sink and was standing with his back to the cubicles, where he could cover both the door and the window.

"So," Jens said carefully. "What, exactly, is going on here?"

Now was my chance! If our gunman was a proper criminal mastermind, he'd be explaining for ages. I zipped off across the tiles in a zigzag pattern.

"I have planted a bomb in the conference room!" he crowed.

"Sounds like a good plan." Jens kept his voice calm. "Why are you holding us hostage in the gentlemen's washroom?"

"Because I thought it was the fire exit. But this ties in perfectly with my plans! When the bomb goes off, I escape in the confusion, and you two take the blame—after I kill you both so it looks like a lovers' suicide pact!"

A whose what now?

But I couldn't pause my scurrying to wonder about that. I finished exactly where I'd wanted to be: between the gunman's feet. A few sharp tugs of my teeth and his shoelaces were tied together. Easy as running through a toilet roll tube.

"And why do you want to blow up the Swedish Embassy?" Lars put in. I wasn't sure if he was buying me time, or genuinely curious.

"I wanted to blow up the Belgian Embassy!" snarled the gunman. "But it was closed for repairs!"

I'd heard enough. It was time for action. He had a nice crease ironed up the back of his trouser leg, which I used to help me scramble up. When the curve of his buttock prevented me from climbing any higher, I followed gerbil agent operating procedure C90 and bit him in it.

I was gambling all of our lives on something I've learned over a long career of popping up unexpectedly: humans, when startled, tend to throw their arms upwards. Sure enough, my target jerked and shot a hole in the ceiling. This was the moment when Jens, or of course Lars, should have rushed him while he was distracted. But neither of them moved. Do they not *show* Bond movies in Sweden?

I jumped, but the gunman's hand was too quick, and I found myself squeezed in his fist. My eyes bulged and my feet kicked uselessly.

"Interesting," he said, covering the Swedes with his gun while he stared down at me. "One of the surveillance gerbil prototypes. I thought they were an internet hoax."

At last! Someone had heard of me! With the aid of my reputation, I'd soon have this terrorist quaking with terror.

And afterwards, I'd work on that line until it sounded a bit better.

"How utterly laughable," the gunman continued. His grip tightened.

"Go pass information to yourself!" I snarled, and I bit down on his finger.

He shrieked and shook his hand. I held on, though the world went blurred. The gunman moved forward, probably to dash me against a basin, but thanks to my cunning work with his laces he tripped and stumbled.

The gun went off again.

The window shattered.

The gunman put out his hand to save himself, but met only air.

I dangled from his finger. Everything was suddenly very loud, cold, and windy.

I wrenched my teeth free, and I fell forever.

"Are you sure about this?" the Old Man asked. Marta carried on adjusting my harness.

"She'll need it now she's been promoted to Surveillance Officer level, and it'll come in useful next time she throws herself off a building."

"I still don't understand how she survived." He rubbed me under the ear.

"Neither do I," I admitted. "Am I a cyborg? Why did nobody tell me?"

"You're small enough to have a non-fatal terminal velocity," Marta explained. "That means you fall more slowly than a human. Your weight's spread out over a wide area when you land, too."

I scratched my chin with a hind leg. Science was less exciting than a hitherto unsuspected superpower, but at least it had saved my life.

"You'll be pleased to know your Swedish friends got the

building cleared, and the army disposed of the bomb." Marta cleared her throat, her eyes not meeting mine. There was something else, something they were keeping from me. Another revelation. Was I getting my damehood? Was the Old Man my *dad?*

"James, we've got something to tell you. *Haven't we?*"

"Go on," I told her.

She glared at the Old Man, who stared at the floor.

"That listening device, the one that looked like a sunflower seed…" he mumbled.

"Yes?"

"It was a sunflower seed."

For the first time in my life, I didn't know what to say.

"I'm sorry, James," the Old Man said. "You were so bored and restless, but my Chief told me my job was on the line if I ever let you anywhere near the field again. You know, after the biscuit tin thing. So we made up a mission for you."

"You utter, *utter*…" I ran out of words again. It was probably for the best.

"It was unforgivable. You almost died." Marta stroked my back.

"But I didn't! I proved myself and my licence to kill has been, um, unrevoked."

"For the last time, James!" said the Old Man. "You do *not* have a licence to kill!"

"But your active status *has* been fully restored, if you're quite sure you want to go back out in the field," said Marta, glaring at him again.

"Or you could retire," the Old Man put in hopefully. "With a medal. And a pension."

"Of course I'm sure!" I drummed my hind feet. "Is it on yet?"

She fastened the last buckle on the harness, tightened the straps, and made a couple of adjustments with a small spanner. "There. Try that out, the way I showed you—*carefully.*"

My paw on the red button at my chest, I gave my whiskers a satisfied flick at the thought of the successful mission behind me, and the many yet to come.

I am James, Secret Agent Gerbil 07, serving Queen and country. And now, I'm a gerbil with a *jet pack*.

14

WORN-OUT TOOLS

The grass rustled.

Bont flicked his ears, and his beady, gentle eyes blinked. Just the wind, blowing across the steppe. He kept walking, aiming for the village below the mountains. His steady three-toed plod had brought him little by little across the vast distance, and he was nearly at his destination.

"Hairy one!"

Bont turned to face the voice, snorting. A young hyena, all legs and teeth, erupted from the grass. Bont snorted again and lowered his head. The forward and greater of his two horns, as long as the hyena's body, sliced his view of the enemy in two. He blew out through his lips.

"Hairy one!" The second attack came from his left flank, but as he wheeled to face it, a third and fourth hyena closed in on his right. The four formed a box around Bont, galloping in to snap at him whenever his ample rear was exposed.

He wheeled and stamped, stamped and wheeled. The hyenas danced around him, and although they backed off when he lowered his head, they were gradually wearing out his strength. Bont tightened his grip on the skin sack he carried. It would have held all four hyenas comfortably, if he could have gathered them into it.

The biggest hyena, growing bold, sprang on his back and clung to his wool. Its teeth gnashed at Bont's hump, but couldn't penetrate the fur and fat. Bont shook it off. It rolled on the ground and jumped back up, thrashing its tail.

Bont broke into a lumbering run. Hyenas bounced off him, scrabbling for purchase. When they grew too close to his front, he swept his horns low, tripping them. In his time he had gored lions with his primary horn; broken skulls with a blow from the shorter secondary. Yelps and hoots accompanied every swing he made. His eyes, made for seeing all around, caught movement everywhere he looked.

They were so fast, moving over the grass like clouds in the sky! The spots and shading of their coats let them hide in clumps of grass or flat against the earth, bamboozling Bont so he could no longer count their number.

The village was close. He aimed his horns at the collection of skin shelters and snorted.

He stumbled as the smallest hyena rushed between his legs. He fell on the trampled pathway with a crash that shook the ground. Dust filled his eyes and his nose. The hyenas, triumphant, bounced on his hump and chased each other up and down his back.

"You cubs stop that!"

The mother hyena spoke in grunts and gestures, but her meaning was clear. The four cubs scattered—the largest was not quick enough, and she smacked it with the side of her muzzle. Bared teeth clonked against its skull. Bont, who reared a single calf each year with his wife and would have died before he hurt it, winced.

"Welcome, hairy one," the mother hyena smiled.

Bont stood, brushing earth from his knees, and followed her to the largest of the skin shelters.

The hyena village was bigger than last year, and it had pushed further north as the steppe receded. It was hard for Bont to see pictures in his mind, but as he looked at the sheets of sunbleached skin, flapping stiffly against branch props, he thought of the deer people, their soft eyes, and the graceful dances they performed.

He lifted the entrance flap and ducked to enter. He sat, and was brought water in a skin bag. The other hyenas came in one by one: the toolmaker, the hunters, and the ones who looked after the cubs. Bont thought there were more hunters, more cubs than before, but he soon reached the limit of his counting.

"I would like some of the small things that hold small things, and a new grind stick," Bont said when he was refreshed.

"Skin pouches and a pestle, got it, got it." The mother hyena nodded enthusiastically.

Since he started his trading visits as a young woolly rhino, the hyenas had changed leader more times than Bont had toes and horns. Back then, he had understood their speech as well as they understood his. Now, they used noises when they spoke to each other that Bont could not follow. The old, simple words and gestures were for cubs, and for him.

"And what do you have for us?" asked the mother hyena. The cubs had come sneaking in along with the adults. The four that were hers, those who had hunted Bont, lolled panting around her.

Bont opened his skin bag. It was hyena-made, and it held many things, more than he could carry even though his hands were large. Inside, smaller pouches held herbs and mosses so they wouldn't get all mixed up.

The hyenas were so smart! They fitted flint to wooden shafts to make teeth that could bite their prey from afar or chew the branches from trees. They made containers so they could carry and store their food and water. They made shelters for sleep, because their hides weren't thick and woolly like his. But they couldn't seek out plants the way Bont could, and they didn't have his nose for separating the ones that harmed from those that healed.

He showed the contents of his pack, spreading the dried plants out or holding the pouch of seeds up to be sniffed.

"For stomachs," he told them by pointing to his own, "for heads, for bones. This one stops bleeding. This one stops wounds going bad. This one stops pain. And *this* one—" His hand hesitated over the small, dark leaves. "This one...stops. When there is nothing more you can do."

They ate, when the bargaining was done. Bont was brought fruit in a stone bowl. The hyena mother conveyed that it was the four cubs who had gathered them for Bont's arrival, when the wind brought his scent to the village. Bont rumbled his approval and patted heads.

The toolmaker brought him what he wanted, and a new thing, too: like a spear, but with a bigger point and short shaft. The toolmaker showed that it was for digging, instead of Bont's horn. Now he could pull up delicate plants without crushing them.

Bont was fond of the toolmaker, who spoke little and watched everything. Like Bont, he looked for things and he found them, but unlike plants, the things the toolmaker sought did not exist until he found them with his mind and made them real.

The smallest hyena cub crept close to Bont and snuggled up against his side. His fingers worked the soft fur of its neck ruff. The cub stretched, splaying its overlarge paws, and laid its chin in Bont's hand.

When stomachs were full and eyes were closing, the mother leaned close to Bont.

"And the other plant?" she asked. "The danger one?"

Gently, so as not to disturb the cub at his side, Bont reached for his bag and brought out the greyish moss with its strong, bitter smell.

"Not too much," he cautioned, breaking off a tiny piece that would suit the light body and quick heartbeat of a hyena.

"Or die," the hyena mother confirmed.

"No. Too much and come back without, without..." He tapped his head, where his mind lived.

She took the supply he gave, and left to conceal it in some secret corner.

The hyena cub slept, its head in Bont's palm. Its ears flicked and its closed eyes crinkled as it dreamed. So many thoughts in a little soft head that Bont could have broken like an egg!

It was warmer here than in Bont's high, far home; warmer than it had been when he first began visiting. Too warm to lie under skins, surrounded by fur and hot breath. He slid his hand out from under the sleeping cub and moved carefully between the sprawled bodies, back through the skin flap into the breeze.

He turned his head so the curved length of his horns caught the setting sun. The forward, longer than his skull, was chipped and worn from a lifetime of uprooting trees, fighting lions, and keeping other men away from his wife.

The horns were heavy, and his wool was heavy too. He lay on the ground and closed his eyes against the orange sun.

He woke to the sound of many paws running, and to yips and yelps of concern. Every hyena was in motion—in and out of the shelters, sniffing and calling. Trying to follow them all with his eyes made Bont dizzy.

When the mother hyena loped by, her eyes wide with worry and her tongue hanging out, Bont stopped her with an outstretched arm and pressed her haunches to the ground. He made her drink from his water bag and he asked what was wrong.

She conveyed that her cub—yes, the smallest, no, not the biggest or the middle-sized ones—was gone. Lost. No scent to follow. The hairy one will help look, yes? He is big and he is good at finding things. The smallest cub likes him.

Bont's eyes and nose were not as good as the hyenas', nor could his legs cover distances quickly. He could travel further than they could, yes, but too slowly to be of use to a lost cub. How long had it been missing? Hyena bodies, warm and small, cooled more quickly than Bont's large frame. And the cub was smaller than small. He wiggled his fingers as if he could still feel the flowerhead weight in his hand.

Bont was not good at seeing pictures in his mind. But he was good with plants.

"I will help," he promised.

He found a quiet spot in the shade, behind the largest shelter. The calls and footfalls of the hunting hyenas were fainter here. He opened his pack and took out the danger moss.

He had warned the mother hyena about it: how it could take you on a journey and return you changed, a shell with the nut gone. Bont had used it as many times as he had fingers and he had always come back, but he could feel that a little of himself was taken away each time, as the pestle that grinds the herbs grinds itself away too.

He broke off a section of the dried moss. Crumbs fell from it to the ground, and he carefully collected them with a damp finger so no cub could lick them up. He placed the moss in his mouth and chewed.

When it was reduced to a wet, dense clump, he tucked it with his tongue between his bottom lip and his teeth. His mouth tingled from the chewing. He settled into a comfortable sit and felt the numbness spread from his lower jaw to his neck and spine. His arms and legs got heavy, and the weight of his horns forced his head down on to his chest.

First he was falling. The ground was above him and he fell into the sky, and it was more frightening than falling the other way because there was nothing there to end the fall.

The world flipped and he was looking down from above. Had a bird of prey taken the cub? Was that the message of the moss? He saw the hyena village below him, and his self, still and calm in the middle of all the activity. With a tug to his stomach, he was lifted higher. Now he could see the whole steppe. There were his wife and this year's calf, tiny as insects but clear in every detail. He reached out to touch them, but they disappeared into the grass.

The steppe shrank. The large people, like Bont's kind and the mammoth, retreated with the grasses, huddling together, dropping in number until none remained. Meanwhile, the hyena village grew, pushing up into the former cold places, and the dancing deer people ran from the hyenas. Soon the hyenas were so many, the deer so few, that the hunters became fighters who killed hyenas from other villages and took their food.

Now the tents in the village lay empty. They fell and disappeared. The hyenas were gone like the mammoth and woolly rhino.

Too far. I need near. I need *now*. He thrashed his limbs, trying to swim back to the hyena village and his body. Instead, the sky over the vanished steppe went from blue to purple to black. Bont was closed in by walls. He stretched his arms and touched rock. At his feet, a small whimper told him he had found the hyena cub.

"I am coming for you," he told it. He tried to pet its ears, but his hand passed through. The cub shivered and tucked itself up even smaller. Its nose was to a crack in the rock, where air and a little light came in.

The cub was alive, but where was it? He pressed himself to

the cave wall, trying to push through. Something caught at his throat and he knew he had swallowed some of the moss.

There was light, so much light. He was outside the cave. With the moss fizzing inside him, there were more colours in the world than he could normally see. Everything was bright and clear, as if the noon sun shone on it.

Where was this place? He didn't recognise it. And how had the little one got in? He looked hard at the rocks, thinking. There was no sign that a cave was there.

Look up, the moss told him.

He saw a fresh pale scar on the side of the mountain, where no plants grew. The moss in his mind told him that part of the mountain had fallen to block the cave entrance and trap the littlest cub.

Who knew that rocks could act that way? The hyenas could picture many things, like skin shelters and stone bowls, but none of them had pictured this. And now he had to get that picture from his mind into theirs. He stared at the mountains. He must hold on to the shape of them, to the landscape around, so the hyenas knew where to go. This was their land, not his steppe.

Bont felt that he had left himself a long way behind. He struggled as if something sticky was holding him down. He sat behind his own eyes, unable to move.

Too deep.

Too far.

Too…

High, faint yips found his ears, and he felt himself being nipped and nuzzled. He opened his eyes and saw a blur, which shaped itself into the mother hyena.

"Hairy one!" she said, nudging him anxiously with her nose. She spoke with movements of her head and paws, and with small noises: she'd thought he was dead! Did he take the danger moss? What about her cub? The scent of her, behind her words, told Bond she feared the cub was dead also.

Alive. Trapped. Let me tell you the place and you can find it. He used his arms to make the shapes he had seen. The picture was already fading from his mind as the moss left him, but the mother hyena was nodding.

"Yes. Yes! We know it! We will go!"

The hunters came with them, although Bont tried to explain there was nothing for them to hunt. The toolmaker, too. And the other cubs could not be kept away. Before the journey was halfway done, Bont was carrying two in his arms. How had the smallest come such a way by itself? It must have walked all night.

There was the mountain with the fresh scar, and there was the cave, and the rock that blocked the entrance. The mother called out, and put her head to the rock. From her face, the smallest cub had called back, but it was too faint for Bont's little ears.

The hunters prowled and sniffed, but could find no other way to get inside. It must be the rock. They put their paws on it. It did not move. They looked at Bont.

Hyenas could not do everything, and that made Bont feel happy. He looked at the rock. It was bigger than he was, and when he put his arms around it, he could not shift it either. It didn't even wobble.

He dug the tip of his forward horn into the earth, as if the rock was a plant he could uproot. The strain as he pushed made his jaws go numb and rigid. This way would not work either.

Bont walked backwards from the rock. He lined it up so his forward horn divided it into two equal parts in his view. He lowered his head.

The mountain echo turned the noise of his feet into thunder as he charged. The rock loomed up, and he closed his eyes.

He struck where he had aimed, the base of his forward horn smacking into the rock. The shock shuddered through his head and neck, and his hump trembled as it absorbed the blow.

Bont stepped back, panting. The rock had not moved. He must start from further away, run faster. He scraped the ground with a foot and paced away, counting one step for each of his toes.

The second strike sent pain shooting through his head, and little bright lights. The rock had not moved. He shook himself and tried again.

The third time, he struck wrong, and the rock tricked him so he fell. His lip was cut and bleeding. The rock had not moved.

It was harder to raise himself after he fell again. The rock had not moved. He staggered as he ran. His ears were full of bird noises and the rock wavered into two rocks. When he struck it and fell once more, the hunters leaped upon him to stop him trying again.

They poured water from a skin bag over his face, and squirted it into his mouth. The mother licked the cut on his lip with her tongue and it stopped hurting. But Bont's mind was full of the cub in the cave. Was it scared by the banging and crashing? Or did it know Bont was trying to rescue it?

The hunters crowded the rock, trying to move it between them. But there was no room for them to push all at once in the same direction. The toolmaker barked at them to stop. When they paid no attention, he came and lay by Bont.

He had the same eyes as the smallest cub, Bont noticed, brown and gentle, and brimming with thoughts. He gazed at the rock, then back to Bont, looking up and down the curved length of the rhino's forward horn. His forehead wrinkled with the strain of all the thoughts behind it.

The mother hyena put her paws on the rock wall of the cave,

as if she could touch her cub through it. Bont watched her, his chin on the ground to relieve the weight of his horns and his aching head.

The toolmaker's paw hovered above Bont's forward horn. The gentle brown eyes asked permission, and Bont nodded. He had no feeling there, so he could not sense the rough pads as they traced the dip and rise of the horn. With gestures, the toolmaker asked Bont to root up a tuft of grass from the soil in front of them.

Bont couldn't see why, but he obliged. Why not amuse the toolmaker? He was useless for anything else. He dug the tip of his horn into the earth and pulled the grass up from it with a tearing sound.

The toolmaker seemed delighted. He jumped up and began searching for something.

While his back was turned, Bont replaced the grass and covered the roots over.

The toolmaker returned with a smooth stone that filled both his paws. He placed it under Bont's forward horn, in the middle where the curve was lowest. He pointed to another tuft of grass.

The job was easier with the stone to rock his horn up and down. Bont understood, and he wanted to try the big rock immediately, but the toolmaker made him wait. He tried the stone closer to Bont's head, then closer to the rock, until he found the place where the balance was best.

Then, with the help of the hunters, the toolmaker found a bigger stone. They rolled it in front of Bont. He rested his forward horn on it and dug the tip under the rock that blocked the cave.

So many rocks and stones and people and places to keep track of! But Bont's task was to lift and push. The toolmaker had given him what he needed.

He rolled his shoulders, sending strength from his legs, weight from his hump, into his head and horn. Resting on the stone instead of the ground gave his horn more room to swing upward, and the weight of the rock felt less.

It was still a great weight, though. Bont pushed until lights floated in his eyes again, bracing his hands and feet against the hard earth. When his feet slipped, the toolmaker scrabbled little holds for them in the ground. He pushed as if he could see the cub on the other side, as if it was his own small family trapped in the dark.

There was a dull crack, and Bont's head jerked. He fell on his side, and in the flashes in his eyes he saw his wife and calf. Something was different and wrong, so different and wrong that he could not tell what it was. He blinked away dust and saw the smallest cub scamper from a black gap in the mountain where the rock had moved.

He was not hurt? In spite of the shock and the noise, his limbs were straight, and he could turn his head.

His head. The white line of his forward horn, like a tree with no branches, was gone from his sight. He saw it lying on the ground, a dead thing bloody at the base where it had snapped away from his head.

Bont had never seen the toolmaker so agitated. The hyena indicated with pats and waving paws that perhaps they could stick his horn back on? Or make Bont a spear, such a good spear, longer than his horn and straight instead of curved?

"No," Bont said. He lifted his head. It felt light, and he raised it higher. He stood straight.

The other cubs were already playing with his horn, jumping over it and chewing it. The toolmaker moved to stop them, but Bont reached them first and picked up this piece of himself, the familiar become strange.

He handled it for a few moments, running his fingers along the chips and scratches. There were pictures in his mind of every fight he had fought, but fighting was for young rhinos.

"I don't need," he said, as much to himself as to the hyenas.

He held the dead thing out to the cubs. They took it in their mouths, fought over it, and ran about with it, their tails high.

The mother hyena's voice was full of love and fear and anger. As she held and licked the smallest cub, she was asking it why. What had made it run from the village and cover such a huge distance? The squeaked and snuffled response was not one Bont could understand.

"She says she wants to be a finder and travel with things to trade," the mother told him, clear and simple so he could understand. "Like you."

15

LITTLE SUN

Personal Diary of Ekaterina Petrova

I've wanted to pet the stray dogs of Moscow ever since I could sit up in my pram, but Papa never let me near them. Now it's my job.

He'd laugh so hard if he could see me running after street mutts with a tape measure, trying to decide whether they're small enough for the programme. His daughter, the scientist.

It's amazing to think of the future that awaits these unwanted, half-starved creatures, if their behaviour is good and they pass all the tests. Like the books I read at school: peasant boys and girls becoming famous heroes through study and exercise, clean living, and loyalty to the State.

The little dog I picked up today was just perfect. She ran to me when I called, pushing her muzzle in my hand. I guess she smelled the sausage I carry. When I didn't give her a treat right away, she cocked her head to the side and raised her front paw as if she had studied a dog textbook on proper begging procedures. How could I resist? Then she stood calmly, eating her snack, while I measured her. All the time she was looking at me with eyes of an intense yellow I had never seen in a dog before.

I lured her round the corner and towards the carrier I had brought. She walked in with total confidence, turned around twice, and lay down. Then into the boot of the car and back to the Institute for a full medical and a flea treatment!

I've named her Solka, Little Sun, for her golden coat and happy smile. It's the kind of name we like in the programme: cute and simple, and a good Russian word, not bourgeois. She's fit, with a calm temperament, and she should go far. Perhaps further than any creature has been before.

But she's so skinny, poor thing! She made me think of the stories Papa used to tell: how, in a harsh winter, humans with the ability to transform took on their wolf form and lived as dogs, coming into the city to beg or steal. This gave them a better chance of finding food, like dustbin scraps, or little girls' fingers.

I stopped believing him when I was eight. When I grew up, I realised he was just trying to scare me out of trying to pet strange dogs. Telling such fanciful stories, even to children, is frowned on anyway.

Mind you, he couldn't resist explaining how the dog required fewer calories because it had smaller mass. Always encouraging me towards the sciences.

I still think of him when I go out after Moscow's mongrels.

And it *was* a harsh winter.

Name of subject: SOLKA

    Height at shoulder: 24cm

    Length: 29cm

    Physical description: No abnormalities or deformities. Docile, placid temperament. Head large, with erect ears. Hair: medium length, soft and golden. Eyes: yellow.

. . .

Personal Diary of Ekaterina Petrova

I'm worried about Solka's weight. She eats and eats but doesn't gain, although we've cleared the parasites out of her and her blood work comes back good.

Her age is a matter for concern as well. She moves like a young dog, and there's no white on her muzzle, but her teeth are very worn, more consistent with an older adult. They're sharp, too; I grazed a knuckle examining her mouth, and drew blood. No biting from Solka, mind, not even a growl.

Her heartbeat is slow for a dog of her size, and her body temperature is lower than I would expect. I measured it at 37° today.

Osokin tells me constantly that I have picked a bad dog, that she will waste our time and resources only to die on us. He puts a special sneer into my surname when he addresses me. Of course, it is Papa's name also, and he was Papa's colleague.

He wants Solka to fail because she is 'my' dog, I think. Certainly, I want her to succeed just to spite him.

Meanwhile, my little golden wolf continues to eat, and to exhibit excellent behaviour. She will sit and lie on command; she must have been someone's pet before she ended up on the streets. Someone who couldn't afford to keep even a small dog any more. Or someone who disappeared.

Whenever I come into the room she jumps up, even if she was sleeping soundly, puts her paws on the wire of her cage, and pokes her nose through. She watches me all the time as I move around the laboratory. When my back is turned, I can feel her yellow gaze. It's a little disconcerting; it makes me think again of Papa and his Moscow werewolves. Dogs with human souls.

To change from a small dog back into a human would displace a large amount of energy, I should think. So, if a werewolf failed to find enough food, they could get stuck on four legs. I never thought to ask about that, which is a shame; Papa would have been pleased with my reasoning.

He would have liked Solka, too, despite his mistrust of strays. I've never known a dog this clever or affectionate.

But if she's not in good health, she won't survive the mental and physical stresses of the mission.

We'll just have to see how the tests go.

Name of subject: SOLKA
   Age: Unknown
   Weight: 4.8kg
   Medical report: Specimen is underweight but physically fit and muscular. Heartbeat 80 per minute, strong and regular. Lungs clear. Teeth worn, but gums healthy.

Personal Diary of Ekaterina Petrova

She's gaining weight! Her coat is longer and thicker, her teeth whiter, and her yellow eyes more intense. The hours I spent going from butcher's to butcher's until I tracked down sheep's hearts have paid off! She looks a bigger dog overall, now!

The graze she gave me with those teeth when I first picked her up has stayed pink and raw, although I took care to disinfect it. But I can't hold that against her. She's such a friendly little thing, and she has never hurt me on purpose, despite everything I have been putting her through.

Yes. We have begun the tests.

It's hard to watch anyone suffer, but it's especially hard with animals. Even a child can understand a simple explanation of what is happening, but a dog knows only that it is hurt or frightened.

Some people think, because of that difference, animals don't have feelings. If I had ever thought that way, Solka's ordeal in isolation would have convinced me otherwise.

We need to see if the dogs can withstand solitude without becoming too distressed, so we keep them in a small room with a one-way window for observation. We left Solka for three days, with food, water, a comfortable bed, even toys. She should have been perfectly happy. But whenever I checked, she was lying just behind the door, staring up at it with her ears cocked for sounds from outside, or else sleeping with her nose to the crack at the bottom.

Dogs do not suffer from loneliness. It is simply that they have an instinctive desire for company because their ancestors formed packs for survival. It is similarly futile and unscientific to credit them with attributes such as forgiveness. Or love.

When I unlocked the door, she ran straight out and into my arms.

The centrifuge test didn't last three days, at least. But Solka's howl from inside the machine, ebbing and increasing like a siren as the capsule spun round, was like nothing I have ever heard before. It was too very human, like a baby's wail, but at the same time wild, unearthly. This time, when I opened the door, she came slowly. I expect she was dizzy. Her yellow eyes looked huge, and flashed in the light. I wished, in that moment, that she had failed the physical; I might have been allowed to take her home with me, as some of my colleagues have done with dogs that failed. An inglorious life awaits them, but a long one, and dogs do not need glory.

Then Solka snuggled up to me, burying her head in my chest. She knows, I am sure, that she is in my power—that I control her movements in and out of all these rooms and boxes. But she trusts me.

Her claws left red marks on my skin where she scrabbled to get close. I must clip them for her.

That's a solid pass in every test! It only remains to acclimatise her to the capsule.

Take that, Osokin!

Solka is going to space!

Name of subject: SOLKA

Heat test: PASS

Isolation test: PASS

Space suit test: PASS

Centrifuge test: PASS

Personal Diary of Ekaterina Petrova

Sometimes, a scientific theory that has been held for decades, centuries even, can fall out of favour. Even the latest discoveries that everyone seizes on eagerly can be suddenly disproved, and the scientists who were formerly praised for their pioneering work find themselves discredited. If they're particularly unlucky, they disappear.

Maybe other beliefs that are unfashionable today will turn out to have been true all along.

What would Papa tell me? Make a hypothesis and back it up with observations. So I have kept a close eye on Solka's behaviour. So much about her seems too good to be true; everyone says how cute she is, except Osokin, who cannot see the dogs as any more than test subjects. Her good table manners; the solemn greeting with outstretched nose or paw; the way she lowers her ears and hangs her head when she realises I have another test for her, then seems to brace herself and go willingly into it. It all looks perfectly natural and doglike —but *too* perfect, somehow. Is she really a dog, or is there a human in there, acting the part of a dog?

It was a small, silly thing that convinced me. When I tested

Solka in the space capsule, she exhibited discomfort. That's not unusual; plenty of dogs dislike the cramped space, the new smells, the feel of wearing the suit, and above all the need to urinate and defecate in it. Some otherwise good-natured and resilient specimens have failed out that way.

My little gold wolf would not even pass through the entry hatch at first, no matter how much I coaxed—even climbing in myself and trying to tempt her after me with her favourite sausage. She stood her ground, her fur bristling, and she growled. Solka never growled at me before.

When I observed her more closely, I noticed it seemed to be a specific panel next to the hatch that was causing her bother. On inspection I found a switch had come loose, exposing the contact behind it.

The *silver* contact.

After I effected a repair, she trotted willingly into this strange new kennel, and chomped her reward.

I was still concerned she might panic, so I got into the capsule with her and closed the hatch from the inside. She watched intently as I opened it again, but made no attempt to follow when I crawled out. I then shut her in from the outside, and the test otherwise ran as normal.

Even if I was correct about what was putting Solka off entering the capsule, there are several potential explanations. She did not like the way the silver flashed in the light, or it smelled funny to a dog's nose. But it stacks so well with the rest of the evidence I have that there is only one thing missing.

I can no longer feel Solka's ribs the way I could when I caught her, and her belly is plump. But she remains, resolutely, a dog. It's just as well; imagine the scandal if Osokin found a girl in the dog pen, naked and with golden hair! She would be arrested as a spy.

Launch date is set for the fifth of April. A full moon. I have seen this small dog increase in strength and power as the moon waxed, enough that it cannot all be down to a diet of sausage and sheep's hearts. What might being alone in the sky with only the stars and moon for company do, for a werewolf who has perhaps stayed a dog a little too long?

The capsule is built for a human cosmonaut; there is ample room inside if it suddenly becomes necessary. The spacesuit will no longer fit, but the suit is more to house the monitoring equipment and Solka's waste than for her protection.

The State has been secretive about the programme, releasing only a few facts, but this discovery—*my* discovery, *my* dog, just let Osokin *dare* try and take credit—will be too big to keep quiet. Think what we will learn on Solka's return, and what we will have done.

We won't have sent the first dog into orbit and brought it back.

We'll have sent the first *human*.

Name of subject: SOLKA

Cockpit test: PASS

Remarks: Solka stood up well to the simulation of space flight: restricted movement, unfamiliar noises, vibration, wearing her suit and monitoring equipment. Her initial reluctance to use the suit's facilities was eventually overcome.

Personal Diary of Ekaterina Petrova

Today I took Solka for a walk.

I wanted to pretend, just for a day, that she was a normal dog like any other. My dog, not the State's.

She was happy to be out of the laboratory, trotting along with her tail high and her little black nose sniffing at everything. But I was unhappy, and she could tell. Gradually she fell back, to walk quietly at my heels, looking up at me with those wolf-eyes of hers.

Space flight is filled with risks, from the moment the capsule door is sealed to the moment it opens again. There are so many ways to die.

Perhaps I am putting my desire to lift my family name out of the mud—so that at least one of the Petrovs might go down in history—above Solka's welfare. But if she is what I think, she must know by now what is demanded of her. With her intelligence, it would have been simple to escape, or mess up the tests. And if she is just another dog, well, we have all hardened ourselves against the inevitable deaths during the programme. Even our spoiled little favourites, because everyone except Osokin has had those.

Our walk took us past the old Church of St Nicholas and, on impulse, I led Solka in. I wanted to see if she had the werewolf's supposed aversion for holy places, and half-thought she might resist and pull away. But, of course, the church was deconsecrated when it was repurposed.

Across the domed ceiling, the constellations sprawl. The swirling Milky Way glows in white, and the other planets of the solar system range themselves in a line.

Solka sat quietly at my feet, gazing upwards as the projected moon cycled through its phases. I wondered if she would howl, but she remained silent. To a dog's eyes, it was just a light on the ceiling. If her eyes are a dog's eyes.

The real moon is almost full now. Solka's golden fur is long and shaggy over a muscled body with surprising weight for its compact size. Her eyes glow.

There is no place for werewolves in the Academy of Sciences of the USSR.

PRESS RELEASE

EMBARGOED UNTIL 05 APRIL

We salute the Soviet Union's smallest hero, who on April 4 became the first living creature to complete a triple orbit of the Earth and return unharmed to her native land.

Little Solka was taken from her struggle to survive on the streets of Moscow to her new role as a brave pioneer. She risked her life in the name of science, for the advancement of human understanding and the glory of the State.

Bravely and patiently she waited for the launch, trembling with anticipation. Observe from the camera footage how calmly she travelled through space, well supplied with food and water! On landing, she greeted her rescuers with happy barks and wagging tail.

Dogs have always gone ahead of their masters, to guide them and to guard against danger. Solka is the guide who will lead us to the stars.

Her mission completed, she will live out her days at the Institute of Aviation Medicine, treated with the respect owed to all our country's heroes.

THE TIMES
   LONDON
   MONDAY APRIL 7 1958

Muttnik Flies Again?

Stargazers in the northeast of Scotland were startled in the early hours of Saturday, April 5th by the sight of a bright, unidentified object in the night sky.

One amateur astronomer was able to calculate the object's flight path, placing its point of origin as the Baikonur Cosmodrome, approximately 1,500 miles from Moscow.

Since the news late last year that the Soviet Union had successfully launched a satellite, Sputnik 2, containing a live dog into low orbit, it has been assumed that further experimental space flights would be carried out, leading to speculation that this was one such experiment.

No announcement has been forthcoming from Moscow, and the Russian Embassy in London declined to comment, but (continues page 5)

Personal Diary of Ekaterina Petrova

I am packing my bags. Whether I will be able to take them with me remains to be seen.

None of us is allowed to know what Osokin saw on the camera feed from Solka's capsule, after he informed me that he would be taking over at my station because I had grown too fond of the dog and might make bad decisions.

As far as I have been able to determine, the film no longer exists. Whatever it was, however, it was enough to make him key in the self-destruct sequence.

His official statement is that the capsule left its plotted course, and would have made a landing outside Soviet territory. We have always known this was a possibility; we cannot let a small thing like a dog's life get in the way of protecting our technological advances.

He knew I was the one who brought Solka in, ran the tests, and passed her. He needs a scapegoat and I was always going to be his first choice.

I presume I am about to find out what happens to disgraced scientists.

All this would be bearable if Solka had lived. I wish I had left her to scavenge in freedom; she did not ask to be made one of science's martyrs. At least she cannot have suffered. Human, dog or mythological creature, nothing that breathes can survive the breakup of a capsule in orbit.

There is one further hypothesis. Osokin is lying.

Evidence? He has lied before, and in similar circumstances: when he was frightened and wanted to save his own neck. He was happy to sacrifice a colleague once. He is likely happy to do it again.

In this version of events, the capsule really did go off course, perhaps by a system failure, perhaps by whatever force was unleashed within it. Who knows what effects—heat, weight, magnetic fields—such an occurrence might have? Osokin lost track of it, and control, too.

More evidence. Osokin has departed for the crash site, ostensibly to search for the wreckage and examine it. But a junior technician would suffice to photograph and gather up the remains of a failed launch.

A dog cannot exit the capsule by itself, and must wait for human help. A human—or something with the form of a human —can work the internal door release. If Solka survived the landing, she will be long gone before Osokin can catch up to her. She could survive, perhaps, among the wolves of the Urals, with her great intelligence and strong will.

This is all wild extrapolation. The simplest answer is always the most likely. There was no werewolf. There is no Solka.

However, a good scientist cannot reach a conclusion until all the evidence is in place.

Here is what I have:

It is the second night of the full moon. My skin itches and burns where Solka's teeth drew blood. My sense of smell is heightened.

"Women's problems", Osokin would say. That is his hypothesis; I have mine. And I am the better scientist. We have both known that, all along.

I know that the last recorded trajectory of the capsule suggests it would have fallen not far from the planned landing site.

I know Solka's scent.

I know that officers are coming for me because of Osokin's lies, like they came for Papa. But if I can be as fast, and as strong, and as *small* as Solka, they will not get me too.

I will find answers.

16

FOR I SHALL CONSIDER MY CAT
J/FRY

"Fry! Fry-Fry! *Felis catus domesticus*, where are you?"

Father Francis walked through the cloisters, clicking his fingers.

"Lost your kitty again?" asked Father Hannah.

"Fry keeps the Lord's watch." He smiled at her and moved on.

As he paced towards the refectory, a favoured haunt of Fry's, the clouds shifted and the sun broke through. Stained glass dappled his habit with patches of colour: the animals went two by two along the windows beside him, progressing from the least to the largest. Emerald frogs, ruby-red foxes, golden lions and leopards, silver rhinoceros approached the Ark in hope and gratitude.

Beyond the monastery and the stained glass animals, the air lay heavy. Those monks whose duties were in the fields moved with bent backs, tending to each sparse stalk of wheat and harvesting the weeds that grew among them—the burdock, sorrel and lady's bedstraw. The older and more infirm transferred pollen from one plant to another with small brushes. They worked in a silence unbroken by birdsong.

By the time Father Francis reached the elephants, the sun was hidden once more and the colours faded from his plain brown robe.

"Evening, Father." The Cellarer looked up from the myco-protein block he was dividing onto plates, ready for dinner. "It's in the pantry. Get it out before I kick it out."

"Of course," Father Francis said.

The pantry was kept dim and warm, with an earthy smell from the growing fungus. The tilapia, for Fridays, floated in their tanks, packed close together and almost motionless. (The wheat in the fields was not for their daily bread. The wheat made beer, and beer made the water drinkable.)

In the gap between the rack of tanks and the floor, two eyes glowed.

Father Francis had painted those eyes, blending greens and blues in a delicate layer across the iris and adding flecks of gold leaf. Now the black pupils were at their fullest expanse and the reflective plate behind them flashed in the light from the monk's torch.

"Naughty puss," crooned Father Francis. "There's nothing down there for you. Come on, then."

Fry emerged, shaking each paw in turn. The spine and tail, comprising hundreds of tiny components, flexed, the hindquarters flattened, and the cat leaped from floor to worktop. Father Francis touched the dimpled pink nose and murmured a blessing upon his creation.

"Boop," he added.

The cat trotted behind him as he returned to his cell, mouth open in a series of demanding meows. A task assigned to the daughter house of St Jerome for the glory of God, and given the three-letter code F-R-Y. Domestic cat (extinct), of the tribe of tiger (also extinct), J/FRY, known affectionately as Fry.

A bed, desk and chair were all the cell contained. Father Francis placed Fry on the desk, grasped the cat's tail at the base and ran it through his fingers. Some of the hairs were out of place, and he took up a tiny pair of pliers to correct them. The tail flicked every time he tried to grab it, and when he trapped it under his hand, the tip still twitched like a separate, living animal.

It was Father Francis who had constructed the cat's skeleton, and programmed the chip that ran it. These were unskilled tasks, usually assigned to a postulant, but he wanted to see his allotted project from conception to completion. He prayed as he worked: *Lord, guide my hand. Grant me patience. Forgive us all.*

When, at last, it was time to clothe the cat's body, he had chosen to make J/FRY a mackerel tabby, the meanest coat a cat could wear. Man had built the angular Siamese and the huge Maine Coon, but God created moggies. The pattern, when you studied it closely, was a complicated thing: the hairs black-tipped and parti-coloured, brown and buff and grey, marked overall with stripes and whorls of black. He gave J/FRY a white bib, tailtip and paws, and a round, homely face. And, very early in the long, long time he had spent on his task, he had begun addressing the cat as Fry.

Father Francis considered himself blessed to have been allocated the cat, and prayed daily for humility, reminding himself that God had made all of his animals equal and placed humankind in charge of them all.

"Spraggly-waggly," he murmured, spidering his hand across the desk. Fry skittered after it and pounced. The monk rolled the cat back and forth as the sprung hind legs kicked. When they disengaged, Father Francis marvelled at the pinpricks of blood on his hands while Fry, all dignity, licked painted coat with dry, rough tongue.

The Abbot visited him before Compline. The hem of his chasuble swayed, and Fry's bottom wiggled. Father Francis placed a calming hand on the cat's back.

"It is completed, then?" the Abbot asked.

"Well, there are still one or two areas to be improved upon. The retraction of the claws, for instance…"

"Father Francis. I have allowed you longer to complete this task than anyone else has taken. Even Father Kozo's pangolin was ready sooner, and you remember how complex that was."

"I do."

"The cat is finished. Just look at it. You will take it to the Ark tomorrow."

"Tomorrow?" The hand stroking Fry's tail squeezed hard, and the cat pulled away.

"I need not remind you," the Abbot said, "that only God can create perfection." He watched Father Francis's blood-specked hand caress and scritch its way up and down the cat's flanks, which moved with simulated breaths.

"No, no, you needn't."

"There's a little verse on graven images in Deuteronomy, too. Though there's not much of the golden calf about this one, eh?" He reached out and tapped Fry's forehead, where the darker stripes formed an M on the cat's fur.

"Some call that the mark of Mary," Father Francis observed, "although it is a mere superstition, of course." The cat pulled away and jumped to the floor, to patrol the dark corners of the room and the space under the bed. The two men watched.

"The workmanship is good," the Abbot allowed, as Fry wove between his legs and pressed the mark of Mary against his shins. "A credit to you, and to St Jerome's. You should be very proud."

"Thank you."

"I wonder what animal we shall find for you next? Something suited to your passion for detail. A butterfly? Or would you prefer to go large and do a peacock?"

"I will be grateful for whatever task I am assigned," replied Father Francis. "The ant, the sparrow, they all have their place."

"Of course. You are excused Vigils to pack for your journey.

If you set out in the morning, and the weather permits travel, you should be at the Ark for Pentecost."

The Abbot turned to leave, and as he turned his toe brushed Fry's flank. The robot could not feel pain, but it could sense when it had been touched. Fry squalled.

"Poor J/FRY," the Abbot said, bending to stroke the cat's electric skin. "Poor J/FRY."

Father Francis's prayers for humility had been answered.

His pilgrimage lasted three days, walking in the mornings and evenings and resting through the midday heat. Just a monk and his cat, pacing out the silent, shimmering landscape, avoiding the overcrowded towns. Father Francis had brought an inflatable dinghy to cross the flooded areas. Fry, claws in, peered over the side of the boat for fish that weren't there, dabbing the algae-green surface with a paw.

Besides the dinghy and a pocket Bible, Father Francis had a sleeping-bag, dehydrated mycoprotein, and tablets for purifying water. Fry needed nothing, not even sleep. The cat's thermodynamic engine was powered by changing temperatures, and so Fry lay in the sun during their rests, or snuggled up to Father Francis when there was no sun, and prowled about at night. When Father Francis woke and reached out for the cat, he would see the green, reflective eyes he had made, moving to and fro in the moonlight as Fry hunted. Fry never gave up the simple faith that there might, somewhere, be prey for a cat.

On the evening of the third day they came to the Ark.

Its proper name was Woodgate Priory, but it was known by many others. The Cathedral of the Creatures. God's Zoo. Animal Abbey. But, most popularly, the Ark. He could hear the bells from the tall and twisted spire, designed to cool the building by funnelling breezes through it, as he approached.

Parched and dusty, Father Francis spoke into the intercom and waited for admittance. He took off his sunhat.

A monk admitted him to the hallway and introduced himself as Brother Will. Their footsteps echoed in the dark, cool space. The arched ceiling was painted with animals: wolves, lions, polar bears. Predators. Their eyes stared down at Father Francis. Beyond the next set of columns it was livestock, sheep and cattle; after that came birds, from the eagle to the wren, frozen in flight.

"You'll want to have a wash before supper," Brother Will stated. "I'll come for you in an hour. It's a bit of a maze!"

The guesthouse had an iron bedstead and a basin. When Father Francis turned the tap, fresh water flowed. He shut it off quickly and prayed his thanks before filling and draining a plastic tumbler four times.

He washed without wasting, using just enough water to make himself presentable. After attending to his own needs, he placed Fry on the bed to brush dust and dirt from the tabby fur. He squeezed each paw so the claws were revealed to their fullest extent, and buffed them to a translucent shine with the pink quick showing through. He had carved those claws from chips of quartz, sifted on his knees from the gravel paths in the monastery garden.

"Are you ready? Leave your animal," said Brother Will on his return. "You can show it to the Archbishop in the morning."

Despite the generous Whitsun feast and the comfortable bed, Father Francis was too excited to sleep much. Fry, charging from his warmth, curled on his chest and purred. He could barely concentrate on Vigils, Lauds or the breakfast that separated the two services. Finally, he found himself at the entrance to the Bestiary, preparing to add his own humble offering to the collection.

The humble offering, in his arms, reached up a paw to bat at the cross around his neck.

He could hear rustling, thumps and strange, exotic calls, but the zoo smell he remembered from childhood was absent.

The door opened and the Archbishop came forward to meet him.

"Your Grace," Father Francis said. The Archbishop stretched out his hand, and Father Francis wondered whether to give the old-fashioned gesture of kissing his ring, but it was only a handshake he was offered.

The Archbishop plucked Fry from his arms and turned the cat upside-down, parting the fur with his fingers and tugging it to check it was firmly attached. He flicked Fry's nose and eyelids, rotated the joints and prodded the belly. Fry, unused to this treatment, went quiet and still.

"We've been waiting for this to finish off the Pets." The Archbishop gestured with his crosier. "We'll add it now—it's all working. And you can have a private tour before the hordes get here."

Father Francis held out his hands. "May I?" he asked.

"Hm? Oh, of course." The Archbishop passed back the cat, and the two men walked through the Bestiary together.

Father Francis paused in front of the tiger, whose coat was a brighter, bolder wash of Fry's tabby. Muscles bunched under the bronze and honey fur as it walked without a sound. Fry, draped round Father Francis's neck, stiffened, and Father Francis felt the static charge as the cat's fur stood on end. He moved to the next exhibit and gazed upwards.

"Magnificent," he said. The archbishop nodded. The elephant blinked small, kind eyes, raised its trunk and shook its head so the broad ears flapped.

Francis reached out to pat the trunk, but his hand struck a wall of clear plastic. "Why do they need cages?"

"Oh, they're not to keep the robots *in!*" The archbishop laughed. "People kept trying to touch them."

Of course. The way they used to touch holy relics, before

those were put behind glass. Did it matter if those old bones, those splinters of the True Cross, were what they claimed to be or a fake, as long as believers believed?

There was the lion, less golden than St Jerome's stained glass beast, but moving and breathing. And alone. The animals went one by one.

"We thought of putting the sheep in with it," said the archbishop, "but we decided that would be too on the nose."

They moved to another section of the Bestiary, away from the exotic, past the fox, badger and deer. The display panels read GUINEA PIG - HAMSTER - DOMESTIC DOG - DOMESTIC CAT. This last pen was empty. Next door, a border collie wagged its tail and followed the two men with its eyes. Father Francis longed to ruffle the long fur and feel the warmth of the artificial skin. Would the tongue be as rough as Fry's when the dog licked his hand?

"Well, Fry? I think you'll be very happy here," Father Francis whispered. The Archbishop looked sharply at him. Fry's claws penetrated his cassock at the shoulder, and Father Francis felt himself glared at from two directions at once. He moved his lips silently, as if praying, and detached Fry from his shoulder. The cat struggled and clung, but Father Francis placed Fry firmly in the pen, with one final stroke from the mark of Mary all along the striped back.

"It won't keep doing that, will it?" the Archbishop asked.

Fry sat in the far corner of the pen, back turned to the men and tailtip flicking. The fur Father Francis had groomed so carefully stood up in offended tufts.

"Fry-Fry?" Father Francis called softly. But the cat would not forgive his sin.

He had lied.

Fry liked to creep about, exploring the hidden corners of the monastery. Fry roamed the long grass in the sun's light. Fry stalked under the moon. Always on the move, in quest of prey. Fry would not be happy in the Ark at all.

But Father Francis had his duty, and the cat had a purpose too. The Bestiary existed so that people might experience a little of what God had created and humankind had lost. Besides, only a human could feel happiness and its counterpart. To think otherwise was fancy at best.

The main door opened, and the visitors poured in. Each left their contribution on the collection plate. Father Francis watched, amused by the way the Church still insisted on paper and coins as the rest of the world moved on. The amounts of money didn't vary, he noticed, according to how wealthy the visitors looked. Then he saw the list of entry fees on the wall. Not an offering, but a ticket.

At the other end of the hall, a monk was setting up toys and souvenirs on a counter. The elephant, visible from afar above the lesser creatures, blinked, raised its trunk, shook its head. The same sequence as before. Father Francis looked at the tiger and saw the groove its rubber-padded paws had worn in the floor as it paced back and forth on one track. The lion, he knew, would have lain down with the sheep if they had been put together.

"This is not a house of God," Father Francis said. "This is a theme park."

"Hm?" The Archbishop paused with his finger on the button that would shut Fry behind the wall of plastic.

"Fry!" Father Francis called, and the cat, for once, came straight to him and jumped into his outstretched hands. "The Lord be with you," he told the Archbishop.

With Fry tucked under his arm, he walked through the gift shop to the exit.

The woman arrived in the middle of the day, when the sun was hottest. She was carrying her younger child, while the older one, a boy, marched determinedly at his side.

The hermitage was isolated, but not so isolated that visitors could not reach it. Father Francis tended the plants that would see him through the winter, his patch of garden increasing every year as travellers brought him precious seeds. He wrote, and he prayed, and he grew older.

Father Francis bent his knees to put himself on the little boy's level. "What can I do for you?" he asked. He spoke gently, but the boy lost his boldness and hid his head in his mother's dress.

"They want to see the kitty," she explained for him. "They wouldn't stop for a nap," she added.

Father Francis welcomed the travellers in to the one-room hut and boiled water for tea. The two children dropped straight away to their knees on the floor. Fry trotted towards them, tail sticking straight up and pink mouth open. The cat brushed and bumped against bare knees; chased an anorak toggle; chewed gently at inquisitive fingers.

Father Francis had often pored over the mediaeval illuminated manuscripts in the library, and he knew that, no matter how intricate the illustrations, how splendid the capital letters, how much scarlet and gold paint had been used, humanity's handiwork could not match the hand of God. But he saw the wonder and adoration in the children's faces, and smiled at their mother.

"We've been to the Ark," she said, and stopped. Father Francis nodded for her to continue. "The animals there—they're not like this."

Fry rolled on the floor, paws waving. The boy reached out to ruffle the soft stomach fur, and Fry's forepaws clutched his hand, claws in. The toddler was lying on her front, grabbing at the teasing tail and laughing.

"What's your secret?" their mother asked.

"The ro—the animals," he caught himself, glancing at the children to see if they were listening, "have artificial intelligence. They learn. I treated Fry as a cat, and thus Fry learned to be a cat."

"Did you have a cat before?" The boy spoke for the first time, without taking his eyes off Fry.

"Oh no! I'm not that old. But I do remember a world with cats in it."

"Come on, you two," the mother said at last. "We need to be back before dark. Now, what do we say?"

"Thank you," both children said, obediently.

Father Francis waved to them from the doorway. When he lowered his hand, it was to cross himself. He asked that the children should grow up strong and safe and kind, and that they would love and cherish all creatures.

He watched as the three figures disappeared into the shimmering evening. What were they afraid of, in the dark? There were no beasts to menace them. Maybe that was it. The stillness. He listened to it until the sun met the horizon. So empty and quiet. Quieter than even he was used to.

"Fry-Fry?" he called.

The shadows were long, and Fry could be hiding anywhere among them. Father Francis clicked his fingers; made a *ps-ps* sound with his lips; tossed a pebble on the ground so it bounced and pattered.

Nothing.

For the first time since the beginning of his voluntary seclusion, the monk felt truly alone.

"Fry!" he called sharply. Was that a rustle? He slowed his hurry to a walk as he rounded the corner of the hut, so as not to scare the cat away. Huge, glittering eyes glared from the shadow at the base of the wall.

"There you are! Why didn't you come?"

A sound came from Fry's throat that Father Francis had never heard before: a rising growl filled with triumph and excitement. The tail lashed. One forepaw, claws extended, rested on a small, damp, furry scrap.

Father Francis knelt down beside the dead mouse, and gave thanks.

ABOUT THE AUTHOR

Alice Dryden's short stories have been published in anthologies themed around sci-fi cats, pirate dogs, animal spies, and sci-fi cats again (sci-fi people sure do love cats), as well as the occasional title not involving animals.

She also writes in the furry fandom under the name Huskyteer and edited The Furry Megapack for Wildside Press.

She lives just outside London with (at time of writing) two gerbils. In her free time, she is probably out on her motorbike, gone swimming, working on a model aeroplane or watching a Bond film.

www.huskyteer.co.uk
@Huskyteer (X)
@huskyteer.co.uk (Bluesky)
@huskyteer@pawb.fun (Mastodon)
(if you come up with a good pun for your online handle, stick with it)

ABOUT THE PUBLISHER

We are a small press publisher based in Dallas, TX. We're LGBTQ owned and operated, and since 2007 we have been publishing stories with queer characters for a niche community. Now we're aiming to bring our stories to the broader speculative fiction community and to find great works from anyone whose voices have been underrepresented in fiction.

facebook.com/argyllproductions
instagram.com/argyllbooks
redwombat.social/@argyll
bsky.app/profile/argyllbooks.bsky.social